Nigel Hinton

Collision Course

Penguin Books

in association with Oxford University Press

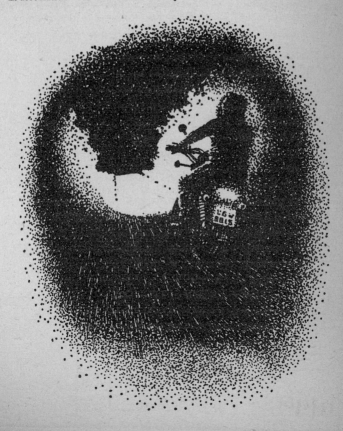

PENGUIN BOOKS

Published by the Penguin Group
Penguin Books Ltd, 27 Wrights Lane, London W8 5TZ, England
Penguin Books USA Inc., 375 Hudson Street, New York, New York 10014, USA
Penguin Books Australia Ltd, Ringwood, Victoria, Australia
Penguin Books Canada Ltd, 10 Alcorn Avenue, Toronto, Ontario, Canada M4V 3B2
Penguin Books (NZ) Ltd, 182–190 Wairau Road, Auckland 10, New Zealand

Penguin Books Ltd, Registered Offices: Harmondsworth, Middlesex, England

First published by Oxford University Press 1976
This slightly revised edition published in Puffin Books 1980
Reissued in Penguin Books 1990
10 9 8 7 6 5 4

To R.G.H.
and the memory of E.K.H.

One

The bike was a dare – not by anyone else, because he was alone, but a dare to himself. The day had been draggy at school. He had drifted from lesson to lesson, half paying attention at first but gradually losing interest and spending most of the time doodling or signing his name. Eventually four o'clock had arrived, and he'd gone back home. He'd enjoyed the walk because the weather was bright and sunny although there was a real winter snap about it.

At home he'd eaten tea, then gone to his room and tried to do some work, but somehow he just couldn't concentrate. He'd played some music, but after one side of some heavy Rock, he'd looked at his other records and just couldn't choose what to play. He seemed to know them all so well – and he wished he could buy something new.

His father came home from work and called out 'Hello', then went to eat in the kitchen. It was then that Ray suddenly decided to go out. He went about getting ready – putting on a thick sweater and his fur-fringed parka – almost without thinking, almost as if he didn't want himself to know what he was doing.

He walked silently down the stairs, opened the front door, and closed it behind him gently.

It was dark and still, and high above the houses the glow from the yellow lights of the main road caught and reflected in a fine mist. He began walking towards the end of his road and turned left. Almost immediately he began to feel better, and he stamped his feet on the pavement to listen to the click echo against the houses. Although it was only just past seven, the back streets were deserted. He turned right, and about fifty yards down the road was the gash of bright sodium light of the main road; he hurried towards it, seeing if he could hold his breath all the way. He reached the end, turned right on to the main road, and gasped in air to his tightening lungs. Out in this yellow glare he felt that there ought to be bustle and excitement, but there wasn't. An occasional car roared by, taking late workers home, but the pavement was empty. He shivered and bundled his hands tight into his pockets and hunched up his shoulders as he headed towards the parade of shops.

He stopped outside a sweet shop and felt in his pocket for a coin to put in the chocolate machine – but he'd forgotten to bring any money and, he discovered, as he felt a drop swell at the end of his nose, he'd also forgotten his handkerchief.

None of the shops was open, and they all seemed dingy and cheap with just one light burning at the back. He looked idly at the advertisements behind the glass-covered notice-board – mostly for second-hand equipment for babies: cots, prams, and toys. Ray looked for one that he'd seen last week offering part-time work as a gardener, but it had gone.

Three shops farther on was the one brightly lit and open place in the whole parade, the launderette. There were three people inside sitting watching their clothes going round in the machines. The bright lights made their faces pale, and they looked bored and tired. He wandered on down the road and came to the pub. There was a low, hooped-iron fence bordering a patch of grass in front of the building, and he jumped it and walked up to the window. Through the net curtains he saw into the main bar and watched two old men playing bar billiards. It looked warm, friendly, and lively inside, and he wished he could go in, but he was young-looking for fifteen, and he knew he couldn't fool anyone that he was old enough to drink. He'd even been turned out of the Astoria once when he and two others had tried to get in to see an 'X' film. The other two had got in O.K. and had enjoyed telling him what he'd missed when he saw them next day at school.

Ray was turning away, thinking that all he could do was wander home again, when a motor-bike drew into the small car-park at the side of the pub. The rider got off the bike, pulled it back on to its stand, leaving the engine running, and walked towards the off-licence bar, undoing the strap of his crash-helmet. He opened the door and went inside.

Ray walked slowly over to the bike. It was a Honda 125 with a yellow tank. The engine sounded good, he noted, and he suddenly felt a temptation to sit on it. He glanced quickly at the bar. He could see the bike's owner standing waiting to be served. Ray ran his hands along the handle-bars of the bike and then swung his leg over the seat and sat astride the machine. He was sitting facing the bar door, and he could see that the man still hadn't been served. Suddenly, he felt the urge to go – to take the bike and ride.

His hand tightened on the clutch, and he flipped the bike into first gear and pushed it forward off its stand. As he stood with his legs astride the machine, he had a moment's doubt about being able to ride it, but then thought about the times he'd been on the back of his cousin Russell's B.S.A., and the two occasions on which Russell had allowed him to have a go himself. Looking up once more at the bar and still seeing the owner's back, he opened the throttle, turned heavily on the handle-bars and began to let the clutch out slowly. The revs of the engine sounded fierce in the car-park and then the bike began to move. Ray lifted his legs, the bike wobbled for a moment as he turned sharply and then he was away.

Without braking, he bumped down on to the road, turned left and accelerated. He changed jerkily into second gear and then felt the surge as the bike began to speed along. He was concentrating so hard that before he realized it he had passed the row of shops and the turning that led to his road and was heading out towards the city centre. He had quickly got used to the bike and found the gear changes quite easy, but he didn't feel that he could yet manage to stop and turn round across the main road. On the other hand, he knew that he didn't want to get into all the traffic of the city centre.

Up ahead of him was the Angel Roundabout, and as he approached it he decided to take the Blackston Road. He slowed at the roundabout, steered the bike over toward the central grass, and cruised smoothly round three-quarters of the circle before drawing out and turning left on to the Blackston Road. It was the most complicated thing he'd done so far, and he felt pleased with the way he'd coped – except that he'd forgotten to signal. Luckily, there had been no traffic. He smiled to himself and flashed the indicators left and right to assure himself where they were.

He lifted himself up off the seat and then sat down again in a more comfortable position. Up to now he had not really been fully aware of what he had been doing – it was as though his mind had been numb. But now Ray felt great. The cold wind was bitter, and he had to keep blinking the tears out of his eyes. He felt a sudden leap of joy in his chest and shouted out at the top of his voice: 'Yah!'

He slowed the bike down and looked back along the road – empty – and there was nothing coming towards him on the long stretch ahead. To test out his control he began to zig-zag from one side of the road to the other. Perfect. Only on the seventh swerve had he even wobbled, and that was probably because the surface was a bit icy. He began to accelerate and again the power and speed sent a charge of excitement through him. He crouched low against the seat, racing-style, and felt the freezing air tearing at his hands and past his head. He began to slow as he approached the straight and leant to take the corner. The bike dipped, and he felt the wheels begin to slide away from him, but he pulled hard and held it up. It had been a close thing.

Farther up the road he could see the lights of the village of Blackston, and for the first time he thought about his position – under-age and driving a stolen bike. He thought quickly about the police and then realized that there wasn't likely to be a cop along this road. Still, there was always the chance of someone else seeing him, so he slowed down and stopped, then began pulling his scarf out of his parka. If he wrapped it round his face and put his parka hood up, nobody would be able to recognize him, and he'd be a bit warmer.

He was still struggling to get the scarf free when car headlights began to shine on him. He ducked his head as the car came towards him from the direction of the village. He bent lower and pretended to be looking closely at something on the bike. To his alarm, the car began to slow down as its lights shone full on him. The police?

The car was stopping. Glancing up, he could see little because of the glare of the headlights. The car drew level with him on the other side of the road. It was small, a Mini. He heard the click as the driver's door opened.

He was just about to thrust the bike into gear and make a break when an old lady's voice quavered over to him.

'Excuse me. Can you tell me whether the petrol station at the Angel Roundabout is still open?'

He mumbled, trying to disguise his voice: 'Don't know.'

'Sorry?'

'Don't know,' he called louder.

'Oh, dear. I'm nearly out of petrol, you see, and I don't even know whether I'll get down there before I run out. The needle is on empty.' Her voice was slightly croaky and a bit posh. She had on an absurd feathery hat.

'Sorry.'

'Well, I'll just have to hope. Thank you.'

She closed the door, and over-revving the engine, she let the clutch out, and the car moved off.

Ray straightened up and settled back on to the saddle. It was all right – she hadn't seen his face. He really must try not to feel and act so guilty.

He finished wrapping the scarf round his face, lifted the

hood, and buttoned it tightly under his chin. It was much warmer and more comfortable except for the faint feeling of dampness on the scarf as he breathed out.

Much more confident now, he slipped the Honda into first and moved gently but firmly away. Protected from the wind around his face and head, he became more aware of the cold on his hands, and he wished that he'd brought his gloves. Wobbling slightly, he pulled the sleeves of his parka down. When he managed it he felt at ease to enjoy the ride fully.

He was approaching the outskirts of Blackston. The houses nearly all had lights on, but the gardens and the road showed no signs of life. Even when he drove nearer the centre and passed the two pubs, there was nobody around. Part of him was glad there was no chance of being seen, but another part of him wanted to be seen – wanted to be thought old enough and clever enough to ride a bike. Finally, near the Clocktower crossroads, he saw someone – a man – walking along the pavement. But he didn't even turn his head as Ray drove past him.

It was nearly eight o'clock by the Clocktower, and Ray decided to drive on for another five minutes or so and then turn round and head back home.

The road out of Blackston was up a long hill which led to the first level of Marpin Plain. When he reached the top, he turned the bike round and paused for a moment, legs astride the bike, looking across to the distant glow from the city. The sight of the far-away lights, and the fact that he was facing the direction home dampened the excitement that had stirred him since he had stolen the machine. The word 'stolen' hit him, and the last glimmer of excitement died. He stood for a moment more, a grey, empty feeling gripping him, and then settled himself on to the bike and set off fast down the hill.

As he rode again through the quiet village, he was planning what he'd do. He would ride back to near his house and leave the bike in a dark road that passed near the industrial estate. It would have to be left there because there were few houses and therefore less chance of his being seen. It was either that, he thought, or leaving it in a car-park somewhere, trying to look as natural as possible.

It had got colder, and the wind even penetrated his parka as he tried to weigh up the advantages of the two plans for dumping the Honda. He was through the village and nearing the bend before the long straight. He changed down and took it slowly, then changed up and began accelerating. The wind increased, and his eyes filled with water, especially when a sudden bump made him bite the end of his tongue.

Out of nowhere he saw the Mini – stopped on the side of the road – its lights off. He began to slow and swing wide to avoid it when suddenly the inside light flashed, the driver's door began to open, and a figure started to get out. In panic he twisted the handlebars and jammed on his brakes. The bike bucked and swerved sideways, and he felt himself falling backwards as it slid away from him on the frosty road.

His right leg hit the road, and he crashed down half on his side and half on his back. Then his head hit the tarmac, and there was an explosion of light and a crack which sounded inside his brain.

He was unconscious as the bike continued its brief slide. He was unconscious as its weight knocked the old lady back against the open car door. He was unconscious as it swept her legs from under her, tumbling her face forward on to its jagged side and scorching her neck against the exhaust.

When he came to, seconds later, he lay still for a moment, then stumbled to his feet. That's when he saw the woman sprawled half under the car and half across the bike. The light from the inside framed the whole scene. Barely conscious of what he was doing, he leant towards her and felt for a pulse.

She was dead.

Two

He'd never seen anybody dead before. He couldn't even pick up a dead bird – death horrified him. And now he ran.

As he ran, the idea hardened in his mind: nobody had seen him, it wasn't his bike, nobody could know it was him, he hadn't any connection with it. Suddenly, the thought burst into his mind – finger-prints! He hadn't been wearing gloves, his finger-prints would be all over the handle-bars. He stopped running and turned back. His head was pounding, and as he walked, he raised his hand and felt the aching bump where he'd hit the road. It was wet – he must be bleeding.

About five yards away from the car, he stopped. The thought of seeing the body again froze him, and then with a shiver of horror he realized that he would have to lift it to get at the bike. With an effort he wiped the thought from his mind and moved round the car, pulling the scarf from his neck.

The old lady was not heavy, but her body was awkwardly trapped under the car door. He tried to roll her, but she was stuck, and he had to pull her by her shoulders to slide her off the handle-bars. As he tugged, he tried not to let himself know what he was doing, but every so often the thought would build up like a scream in his head, and he would want to shake himself free from the act and run. Finally, he could get at both the handle-bars. Kneeling down, but turning his head away from the body, he began to wipe the cold metal and the rubber grips with his scarf.

It was because his head was turned towards the road that he saw the headlights begin to appear round the bend. Another car was coming. With his mouth open and his body in a tight knot, he jumped to his feet. There was no time to get away down the road. He ran across the road, jumped the ditch and plunged into the woods opposite the car. Branches pulled and stabbed at him, but he ploughed his way through them for about fifteen feet and then fell to the ground.

As the headlights grew brighter, he heard the car slowing down. Ray squirmed himself round in the dark wood, crawled behind a tree and lay there looking out towards the Mini and the tangled bike. With a lurch of his heart he saw some red-and-white stripes beside the crumpled figure. His scarf – he had left his scarf by the body. Again his brain swelled inside his head as though it would explode.

The car door clicked open. 'Oh hell!' It was a man's voice. Then as another door clicked, 'No, no. Don't get out – you stay there.'

Still Ray could only see the headlights of this car shining on to the Mini. Then a man appeared. He was walking slowly towards the bike and the body. He was walking with one hand out; it was as though he was unwilling to look, and his body was turned sideways as though to make a quick break for it if necessary. Ray could see him clearly. He was middle-aged, wearing a dark blue overcoat. He bent down towards the body.

'Oh no, it's Mrs Chalmers. Christine, it's Mrs Chalmers.'

'Is she dead?' called a voice from the car.

'I don't know.'

Please don't see the scarf. Please don't see the scarf. Go away. Ray buried his face in his arms. When he raised it, the man was standing looking down the road. He turned and started walking back towards his car.

Please go away.

'Is she dead?' said the woman.

'Yes.'

'Oh, no! What shall we do?'

'You take the car back to the village and get some help. I'll stay here.'

'No!' In his despair Ray almost spoke out loud.

'Please come with me. Don't stay here. I'm shaking too much to drive.' Her voice trembled.

Ray gripped the earth with his fingers and prayed that the man would agree.

'Please – there's nothing you can do here.'

'All right,' said the man.

Ray heard the two doors slam and the car being started. The headlights shone in through the trees as the car began to turn round and Ray hugged the ground, although he knew that he was well hidden. The car began to drive off up the road towards the village.

When he could no longer hear the car, Ray got up and ran out on to the road, picked up his scarf, looked round to make sure that he hadn't left anything else, and then started to run down the road away from the village in the direction of the roundabout.

His head pounded and the cold air burned his lungs. He tried to calculate how far it was to the main road. About three-quarters of a mile. How long would it be before the police arrived? Would they come from the village or would they come from the city?

He was dimly aware of pain in his right leg, in his back and in his head, but with these questions racing through his brain he was not really conscious of the effort of running, and he kept a steady speed, occasionally looking back over his shoulder down the long road. There was no activity back by the Mini, and each time he looked round, the scene was farther away and more shapeless. Soon, all he could see of the car was the light from inside, like a single eye far away in the dark. Then he reached a bend, and the car was out of sight.

He slowed to a walk, gasping for breath and holding the pain in his side. The cold air had torn at his lungs, and he felt sick, but he walked quickly. Then, as he rounded another bend, the bright lights of the main road and the roundabout came into view a couple of hundred yards away. At the same time he heard the siren from the direction of the city.

With a re-awakening of panic he started to run again. A five-bar gate loomed ahead and he climbed it into a field, crouching low behind the hedgerow as the siren grew louder. Headlights lit up the road, and he saw the flashing blue light of the police car rush past. As soon as it had gone, he stood up, climbed over the gate, and ran towards the bright lights of the main road. There he slowed, and tried to walk calmly and normally. He turned left and walked along the verge. About fifty yards on was a bus-stop with a wooden shelter, and as he reached it and ducked inside, he heard the sound of another siren. He looked out and saw an ambulance drive round the corner and disappear up the Blackston Road.

He sank back into the shadows of the shelter and leant against the wall. His knees were trembling, and he felt cold as the sweat began to dry on him. He closed his eyes and tried to block his mind to any thought, but jumbled pictures kept forcing themselves on him – although they seemed to have nothing to do with him, as though he was seeing what had happened to someone who wasn't really him.

Cars passed in both directions, and he watched them remotely as they turned round the grass mound of the Angel Roundabout. One or two of them stopped at the petrol-station on the far side on the City Road, and he was suddenly reminded of the old lady asking him if it was still open. If only she hadn't run out of petrol . . . if only he hadn't nicked the bike . . . if only . . .

For a moment it seemed that if he wished hard enough, it would all go away – just like the feeling he had sometimes that it wasn't impossible for him to go back into the past and be part of the historical events that he read about. Just like the feeling he used to have when he was a kid, that he could fly if he really wanted to. He remembered the dreams he'd had about flying – they were always the same. He would run backwards, flapping his arms, then lean into the wind, and with no effort, easily, the ground would fall away from him, and he would see his garden below as he hovered in the thick air.

He jerked himself out of the memory and tried to concentrate on what he should do. The most important thing was to get home. He'd have to be seen on the bus – it was too far to walk in his weakened state. He looked down at his jeans. There was a rip at the right knee, and he could see that the skin inside was badly grazed. He took off his parka. There was a small tear on the shoulder, and some blood on the inside of the hood. He felt the back of his head. It was tender and there was a large lump, but it seemed to have stopped bleeding although he could feel that the hair was matted. He would have to keep his hood up. If he could act naturally and not betray any signs of panic, he should be able to get away without being noticed.

He put on his parka, brushed it down, and pulled up the hood. As he did so, he saw a Number 53 bus turn down towards him. He stepped out of the shelter and held out his hand. As the bus drew up, he noticed how bright it looked inside. Keeping his head down, he stepped on and climbed the stairs.

There was no one on the top deck. He sat down in the back seat. As he settled he heard another siren, and through the back window he saw the ambulance, blue light flashing, draw out of the Blackston Road. It circled the roundabout and sped off towards the city. Ray watched it disappear from sight, moving fast and sounding its siren. With a sudden surge of hope, he wondered whether the old lady was alive. Surely they would only drive like that if they wanted to get her to hospital quickly. Please, let her be alive.

He looked round again, but as he did so, the hope died within him. He knew she was dead. There had been no pulse, and the man in the car had seen that she was dead. There was no hope there – the only hope lay in not being found out. He must get home, and he must get there without being noticed. She was dead and there was nothing he could do about it. Even if he told someone what he had done, he couldn't bring her back to life.

Two stops before his, he heard the conductor coming up the

stairs, whistling. Ray pulled the hood further over his face and felt in his pockets for his fare. There was nothing in his parka, and he was just squeezing his hands into his jeans when he remembered he had no money on him – he had found that out when he had wanted to buy the chocolate.

The conductor was standing beside him. 'Fare, please.'

The skin on his face tightened, and his mind spun. Stay calm, stay calm.

'Five, please,' he said, reaching into his jeans pocket.

The conductor twirled the handle of the machine, tore off the ticket, and held it out to him. Ray pretended to search his parka pockets again.

'Oh, blimey, I've left my money at home,' he said, turning his head slightly, but keeping his face down.

'Come on – don't give us that.'

'Honestly, I must have left it at home.'

'I've heard that before. Come on, pay up.'

'But I haven't any money.'

The conductor paused. 'Well, in that case, you'll have to give me your name and address.'

'Look, I'm sorry. I'll get off now.'

'It's a bit late for that, isn't it? I've given you a ticket. I've got to account for all the tickets at the end of the journey.'

'But I haven't got any money, honest.'

'Well, in that case, you'll have to give me your name and address.'

'But it's only five pence,' Ray pleaded.

'I don't care about that.' The conductor got out a notebook and pencil. 'Name?'

'John.'

'John what?'

'Timpson.'

'Address?'

Ray thought quickly of a road near his school. 'Sixty Barnford Road.'

'Barnford Road?'

'Yes.'

'Right – you'll be sent a bill by the company.' The conductor began to turn away. Ray got up quickly and followed him down the stairs, pausing only to ring the bell.

The bus was slowing when he reached the platform, but the conductor grabbed his arm and pulled him round. The movement caught him by surprise, and the conductor looked directly in his face before Ray ducked.

'And don't ever get on a bus again unless you've got the money. Understand?'

'Yes. I'm sorry.'

The bus had stopped and Ray jumped off as the conductor let go of his arm. The bus moved off and Ray realized that he'd got off one stop too early. He began to walk along the road towards his turning, tears filling his eyes. He had been seen, and the moment the police started an investigation, that conductor was bound to remember him.

He stood, dazed, then walked across the road, brushing the water from his eyes. Whatever else, he had to get home.

He began to run.

Within minutes he was outside his house. The light in the front room was on, they were watching TV. He felt for his key, opened the door quietly, and crept up the stairs into his room. Without turning on the light, he locked the door and fell face down on to his bed.

Three

It must have been well over an hour later that he heard his parents coming upstairs. He was surprised when he heard a knock on his door and saw the handle being turned.

'Ray,' his father called. There was a pause, then louder knocking. 'Ray, are you in?'

He had wanted to pretend he was asleep, but when his father knocked and called out again he called back:

'O.K., just coming.'

As he raised himself from the bed, his head pounded and hurt. He pulled off his parka and threw it on to the chair, then he kicked off his shoes, undid his belt, and slipped out of his jeans.

'Ray?'

'Coming.' He put his dressing-gown on over his clothes and had his hand on the door handle when he remembered the bed. He pulled back the blankets, messed up the pillow and sheets to make it look as if he had been sleeping. Then he opened the door.

His father stood framed in the light from the hall. With a sense of shame and disgust Ray could feel himself shaping his face to look as if he had just woken up.

'Oh, you're in, then.'

'Yes, of course I am – what do you mean?'

'Well, you weren't in earlier, were you? And we didn't hear you come in. So I wondered if you were still out.'

'Oh no, I only slipped out for a quick walk. I wasn't gone more than about twenty minutes.'

'Well, there was a phone call for you earlier, and your

mother couldn't find you anywhere. You ought to let us know if you're going out or anything. I mean, you don't have to tell us everything you're doing – we don't want to be nosey, but it would be nice if you just said you'd be popping out or whatever.'

'Yes, Dad. I'm sorry, I didn't think.'

'Yes, well – next time, eh?'

'Yes, Dad. I'm sorry. Really.'

Ray wanted to cry. He wanted to be able to reach out and tell his father what had happened. He wanted to throw off all his problems and let his dad sort them out as he had done in the past. But he couldn't. It hurt him to grow away from his parents and he knew that it hurt them – especially his dad. Sometimes, he could see a questioning look in his father's eyes when he said or did something, but sensing the barrier between them, his dad now never asked the question.

Ray looked at his father, aching to be able to tell him, but his self-hatred stopped him. He didn't want his father to know what he had done. He still wanted his father to love him as he used to – the clean, innocent boy who didn't have a secret world of lies and fears.

'Ray, is anything up?'

'No, why? What do you mean?'

'Well, you don't look well . . . I mean you look sort of . . . I don't know . . . sort of worried . . . and not well.'

'No, I'm all right. Blimey, Dad – you've just got me out of bed. Of course I don't look great.' Ray was amazed how good he was at lying – he'd even managed to make that sound like a joke.

His father laughed. 'Yes, I'm sorry. I don't suppose I look too good first thing, either.' He paused – he obviously wasn't totally sure. 'Anyway, if anything needs to be sorted out, you'll let me know, eh?'

'Yes, of course. But there's nothing, honestly.'

'Right then. 'Night, Ray.'

' 'Night, Dad.'

He closed the door as his father turned away, and the guilt and grief that he felt burned his face. He put his hand to his forehead – it really was hot, perhaps he had a temperature. He took off the rest of his clothes and put on his pyjamas. His body ached, and he knew he ought to wash his grazes and cuts, but he didn't want to draw attention to himself by going to the bathroom.

He eased himself into bed and pulled the covers over. He couldn't lie on his back because his head hurt if he put any pressure on the bump. His mind was buzzing with thoughts. He tried to stop the confusion and think logically.

Nobody had seen the accident. He had wiped his finger-prints from the bike. He had got home. Surely he was safe? Where were the dangers? Someone might have seen him steal the bike, but that wasn't likely. His whole journey had been along empty streets, and nobody would have recognized him from a car. The bus – there was a real danger. He had got on at the Angel Roundabout, only a mile from the accident; he'd been seen by the conductor, although only briefly, and he'd given a false name and address. Nobody would be able to trace him through that – would they?

He tried to imagine the police investigation: stolen bike; no finger-prints; no witnesses to the accident; no witnesses to the theft. They would question the man and woman in the car, but they hadn't seen him. The scarf? Even if the man had noticed it, there must be thousands of red-and-white scarves. But if he had noticed it and later had seen that it was gone, then the police would know that the motor-cyclist had returned to the accident. It would also mean that they knew the time, roughly. They'd be bound to check all the buses. Would they find out about the boy who had got on the Number 53 at the Angel Roundabout and who had given his name as John Timpson? Would they check up and find that it was a false name and address? So what? They would still be no nearer. Or would they? Barnford Road was near his school – would they come to the school and start asking questions there? Could he lie to them successfully? They weren't like his parents. They knew how to trap people when they were lying. He had an alibi – he'd been at home. His parents would support him about that. They believed that he'd only been out for twenty minutes. Or did they? His father had noticed that things weren't right.

Oh, hell, the whole thing was so full of possibilities, things that could go wrong.

And all the time the picture of the old lady kept swimming into his mind. She was dead, there was no doubt about that. And he had killed her. It was an accident, but it had happened really because he hadn't known how to ride the bike properly, a bike that he had stolen, that he had been riding without a licence.

He felt himself begin to slip towards sleep and he let himself go, gratefully, into the blackness where he wouldn't think, where he was not guilty of killing someone.

Four

He must have been sleeping very lightly, because he knew it was a dream, but he couldn't stop it, and it didn't seem any the less real. It was in a seaside town, and it was cold – so cold that a barrel of water at the back of the Chinese restaurant was frozen solid. And the body was in the ice a few inches below the surface – you could see it suspended as though trapped in glass. Ray and his brother Derek had put earth on top to cover it up. They were both trying to live their lives normally. He kept talking to Derek to make sure that the young boy knew that he mustn't mention the body in the barrel.

Then suddenly it was all taking place in a Canadian lumbertown and it was spring and growing warmer every day. The roads were turning muddy as the warmth melted the winter ice, and water was beginning to seep out of the barrel. Soon the body would float to the surface, and the bald head of the man would appear through the mud on the top of the ice.

Derek was talking to a Royal Canadian Mounted Policeman, and Ray knew that the Mounties always got their man. Derek was being clumsy in his attempts to cover up the murder. Ray could hear him saying, 'There isn't a man hidden in the ice in a barrel in the back-yard of the Chinese restaurant.'

And the Mountie was sitting on his horse saying, 'Isn't there? That's all right then – but I'd better take a look.'

And the icicles on the roof were melting, and Derek was only eight years old, and Ray knew that the little boy was making terrible mistakes in everything he said, and that soon their crime would be discovered and there was nothing they could do about it. And Ray could see the Mountie riding down the muddy road past the timber-yard towards the Chinese restaurant, and he wanted to run away but he couldn't leave Derek.

Five

He woke up sweating and threw the covers off himself and sat up. It was still dark, but a grey light was beginning to filter through the curtains. He knew that it had been a dream, and he also saw the meaning of the dream. But the horror of what he was really guilty of pressed down on him and made the dream seem silly.

He sat for a few minutes shivering and then lay down and pulled the covers right up over his face. The bump on his head was still very sore as he turned on his side. The minute he closed his eyes, memories of the night before flashed into his brain, and he saw the car with the door open and the light shining down on to the old lady's body. He opened his eyes and tried to concentrate on something else, but nothing would come. The old lady – what was her name? He was beginning to find it hard to breathe under the blankets, and he poked his head out into the darkness of his room.

He peered at the far wall through the gloom, trying to make out the pattern on the wallpaper, but he knew that was simply an attempt to keep his mind off the accident. It was no good – he would have to let it tumble through his mind. What was her name? The man had called it out to his wife. Cathcart? It was something beginning with C. Cathcart – it sounded like it. Other names beginning with C began to play around inside his head. Crumble. Cross. Crashaw. Chump. Stupid names – almost like jokes. How could he be thinking of silly names when he was trying to remember the name of someone he had killed? Cathcart – it must be that, because it kept coming back to him.

*

When next he woke it was morning and he could hear sounds of running water from the bathroom opposite his room. He looked at his watch – 7.15 – much earlier than he usually got up. He must try not to arouse any suspicion by acting strangely, but he simply could not lie in bed thinking about what had happened.

He pulled back the bed-clothes, sat up, and examined the graze on his knee. It had dried during the night, but there were shreds of skin hanging loose, and when he tried to pull them off, the pain made him aware of the bruises and swelling along the outside of his leg. He stood up and put his weight on the leg. It was painful, but it would be all right once he got it moving. The same with his back and neck, which were stiff and sore.

He turned back and looked at the sheets for blood-stains. Nothing, but the pillow showed brown smears of dried blood. He pulled the pillow-case off and stuffed it into the pocket of his school trousers, then dressed quickly. He picked up his jeans from the floor and looked at the tear – it was big, he'd have to tell his mother that he'd ripped them playing football and ask her to mend them. Then he checked his parka – he'd have to get the blood-stains out of the hood, although they were very faint on the dark green material, but he'd try and sew the small rip on the shoulder himself – no point in drawing his mother's attention to that as well. He folded it up and tucked it underneath his sweaters in the bottom drawer of his wardrobe. Then he opened his door slowly.

'Hello, you're up early.' Ray jumped with surprise at his father, who was standing outside his door. 'I was just going to give you a knock to wake you up.'

'Yeah, I've got to get to school early today.'

'Oh? What's special?'

'Nothing – I just want to see some people about some work I didn't understand.'

His father smiled. 'Well, it's nice to see you so keen. I'll tell your mother to get your breakfast on.'

'Thanks.'

His father started down the stairs, and Ray walked quickly to the bathroom and locked the door behind him. In the mirror above the basin, he looked pale and red-eyed and tired. With his mother's hand-mirror, he examined the bump directly at the back of his head. The hair was matted with dried blood. He filled the basin with water and used his flannel to wipe the hair and the bump clean. He dried his hair carefully so as not to start the bleeding again.

Using soap, he scrubbed the pillow-case until the stain was too faint to be detected, then wrung it out. The area that he had washed would dry out on the pillow.

After he had washed himself, he spent a longer time than usual brushing his hair and trying to make himself look tidy. When he had finished, he gazed closely at his reflection. His eyes still looked bloodshot, and he was so pale that the wisps of fluffy beard that were beginning to appear round his chin stood out clearly. Normally he was quite proud of what he called his 'beard', which his father referred to as 'fuzz', but today it only concerned him as a contrast to his paleness; he didn't want his parents to notice anything and start asking questions.

The handle of the door rattled, and Derek's voice called:

'Who's in there?'

'It's me.'

'Well, hurry up, you've been ages.'

'O.K., won't be a minute.'

'Come on, I'm busting.'

'All right.' Ray's voice was hard and irritable and he thought immediately that he must be careful not to let his anxiety show by snarling at people. He stuffed the pillow-case into his pocket and opened the door.

'At last!' Derek rushed past Ray, still dressed in his pyjamas.

In his bedroom Ray put the pillow back into the pillow-case and laid it down on the bed with the damp side upwards so that it would dry more quickly. It looked creased, but at least there were no signs of the blood.

As he went down the stairs, he noticed that the newspaper wasn't in the letter-box – his father must be reading it. Ray desperately wanted to see if there was any news about the accident. In the kitchen his father was sitting at the table with the paper in front of him. His mother was standing at the sink washing up.

'Hello, Mum.'

'Good morning, dear. Your egg's nearly ready. Do you want cereal first?'

He didn't feel hungry and didn't really want to eat, but he was determined not to do anything to disturb his routine.

'Yes, please, but I won't have any toast.'

'Right. Is there enough tea in the pot, Bob?'

His father leant across the table and lifted the lid.

'Yes – it should be hot. I've just had a second cup.'

Ray sat down and poured some cereal into the bowl, added milk and sugar, and began to eat. His father turned to the back page of the paper and held it up to read. From across the table, Ray scanned the front page. There was nothing there. He was anxious to look through the whole paper and he felt his temper rising as his father methodically read the sports news. Ray turned the cereal box and began reading that instead.

'Your egg's ready,' said his mother, putting it into his egg-cup.

'Thanks.' The egg was perfectly cooked, but Ray ate it mechanically and with little pleasure as he waited for the newspaper.

'It's a quarter to eight, Bob.'

'Right, dear.' His father folded the paper and put it on the table, got up and went over to his wife. He kissed her on the cheek and said, 'See you later. 'Bye, Ray.'

' 'Bye, Dad.'

His father left the kitchen, and his mother turned back to the sink. Ray picked up the paper casually and started turning the pages, glancing quickly at all the headlines. On the third page there was a big story about a crash, but it was about two lorries that had collided on the M.1. Then at the bottom of page six he saw the headline –

'Hit and Run Death.'

It simply said:

'An elderly woman was knocked over and killed by a motor-cycle last night near the village of Blackston, Leics. The driver of the motor-cycle, which had been stolen, failed to report the accident. Police investigations are under way.'

Ray read it three times, and the final sentence ran in his head like a bell of doom. He looked at the headline again: 'Hit and Run'. It sounded like a game until the last word – 'Death'.

'Did you hear me, Ray?'

'What?'

'I asked you whether they won,' said his mother, turning round and looking at him.

'Who?'

'Your team – weren't they playing last night?'

'Oh yes. I haven't looked.' He turned quickly to the back page and looked down for the football results. 'It was a draw. Two, two,' he said.

'Are you losing interest in them, or something? It's usually the first thing you look at.'

'No, I just forgot that they were playing last night, that's all.' His mother was staring at him. He felt a blush creep upwards from his neck. She looked as though she was going to say something, but then she turned back to the sink and began to dry up a plate.

Bad – he had been careless. This was hard to keep up. There were so many mistakes to avoid, it seemed impossible to act naturally. For a moment he wanted to get up and tell her – to let her know his awful secret. But even as he thought of doing it, he knew that he couldn't. Instead, he finished his egg and then got up and said as brightly as possible:

'I'm off to school now. I've got to get in early to sort out some work I couldn't do. 'Bye, Mum.'

' 'Bye, dear.'

He ran up to his room for his jacket and his case, then started down the stairs again. Derek was just entering the kitchen door as Ray began to pull on his raincoat.

'Ray!' his Mum called.

'Yes?' He went to the kitchen and stood in the doorway.

'Two things. First, Dave Fitzroy rang last night while you were out – he didn't say what he wanted. Second, are you coming straight home from school this evening?'

He thought quickly. 'I expect so – why?'

'Well, I'm popping into town to see Grandma, and I wondered if you'd get one-and-a-half pounds of sausages at the butchers – save me going out of my way.'

'Sure.'

'Thanks.' She picked up her purse from the sideboard and gave him a pound. 'Don't forget, will you dear?'

'O.K.' He turned to go.

'You're going early, aren't you?' said Derek.

'Yes,' Ray said, and thought, 'Don't rub it in.'

He pulled the front door shut and breathed deeply. The strain of all the lying and anxiety was enormous. How long could he keep it up?

Six

It turned out to be easier at school. From the first moment of his arrival, the sense of movement and bustle helped take his mind off the thoughts that had haunted him for the last twelve hours. In fact, he discovered that he really did have some work to catch up from the previous evening. As he mentally crossed off one lie he felt a momentary sense of relief. By the time he'd finished copying out his geography notes, the first bell had gone, and he plunged himself into the activity of the day.

In the morning's lessons he paid much closer attention than usual, and made a great effort to ask questions and understand what was being said. Easiest of all was the chemistry lesson in which, almost for the first time ever, he pushed himself to take an active interest, really trying to get the experiment right instead of mucking about and missing the point. When the bell rang for lunch-time, he felt pleased with his morning's work and the way in which he had kept his mind free of his worries.

The lunch-break was not so easy. Usually he and a group of friends left the school and went to Ian Turner's house. Ian's parents both worked, and since it was only two streets away from school, it was a convenient place to go for a safe smoke during the dinner-hour. Ray didn't like smoking all that much, and he rarely joined the others as they puffed deeply; but he enjoyed getting away from school, having a few laughs and listening to some music.

Today, they decided to get some chips before going to Ian's place, and they all headed to the fish and chip shop. It wasn't until they reached the street where the shop was that

Ray remembered it was Barnford Road. The whole incident on the bus came flooding back, and as they turned the corner in a group, he hesitated and looked down the road. He realized that it was unlikely, but he was scared that there might be a police car checking up on the false address he had given. He couldn't even remember the number of the house that he'd given, though a quick glance told him there were no police cars anywhere along the road. But the damage was done – the fears came pouncing back, making his heart beat fast and his mind whirl with panic.

He followed the others across the road and stood behind them in the queue along the counter of the shop. They talked and jostled one another and shook salt and vinegar on to their chips, while he watched and felt an enormous gulf open up between him and them. They seemed united in their happiness. Their worst worries were whether their school work was finished on time, or what sort of mark they would get for it, whereas he ... Just yesterday, he'd been like them, but now he was trembling on the edge of being discovered by the police.

The smell of the frying began to clog the back of his throat, and he felt a wave of sickness surge up. He turned from the counter and lurched through the doorway into the street, and by walking quickly and breathing deeply he managed to dispel the sickness. As soon as he began to feel better, he realized how stupid he had been. He slowed and looked down the road – everything looked grey and dull and he felt lifeless and exhausted and he wanted to sink into a deep sleep.

'Ray!' The shout came from behind him. Dave Fitzroy was running along the pavement towards him.

'Where are you going?'

'I dunno – I just suddenly felt sick and had to get out of there.'

'Yeah, you look very pale. Are you O.K.?'

'Bit better. I thought it would be best to walk around a bit.'

'Why don't you go home?' Dave's face peered at him, worried.

'No, I'll be O.K. Aren't you going to Ian's?'

'No, I'll stick with you.'

Ray felt grateful for Dave's concern and the 'I'll stick with you' was a really nice thing to say. They walked along the road together, in silence, Dave eating his chips.

'I phoned you last night,' Dave mumbled through his last mouthful. He screwed up the empty packet and dropped it in the gutter.

'Yeah. I went out. What did you want?'

'Nothing. Just a talk.' Dave paused and looked at Ray. 'You feeling better?'

'Much.'

'Where'd you go?'

'When?'

'Last night.'

'Oh, just wandered around.'

'Hey, I need a fag. Let's go to the park.'

They turned down Prendergast Street and into the park. It was a flat, open and unattractive stretch of grass next to the cemetery. It was empty except for a woman wheeling a pram across on the far side. They sat down on a bench, and Dave pulled out a packet of cigarettes and put one in his mouth, then offered the packet to Ray.

'You smoking today?'

'No, thanks.' Dave started to put the packet away. 'Yes. O.K. I think I will.'

They sat together smoking, just looking across the grass. Ray liked the fact that Dave was someone who you could be silent with – you didn't feel the need to talk all the time. They had known each other since the first year of Secondary School and Ray had always considered him to be his closest friend. Perhaps he could trust him. He leant back and said:

'Dave, what would you do if you were in trouble?'

Dave laughed. 'I'd say I'd never touched her.'

It was only a joke, and one that Ray would have made yesterday, but it just seemed so stupid and so typical of the sort of juvenile attitude that all of the kids of his age had that he knew straight away that he couldn't posibly look for any help from his friend. He threw his cigarette away, half-smoked, and got up.

'Why, what's up? Are you in trouble?'

'No, of course not.'

'Well, why did you say that?'

He lied quickly – God he was getting good at that. 'I just thought about you ringing up last night and I wondered if you'd wanted to say something to me.'

'What about?'

'I don't know – and it just suddenly occurred to me whether you would tell me if you were in trouble.'

'Of course I would.'

They headed back towards the park exit.

'First I'd tell my parents, then you.'

Ray kicked a stone and ran after it, then turned and kicked to his friend shouting, 'Goal!'

'Never. I pulled off a fantastic save.'

Ray laughed, and the moment passed, but as they headed back to school with Dave chattering on about things, he felt more lonely than ever.

Seven

During the first afternoon lesson, everything seemed to be combining to remind him. His knee began to itch as the graze healed, and the history teacher chose that day of all days to tell them about Sir Robert Peel and the development of the police force. In direct contrast with the morning, Ray tried not to listen and began doodling in his rough notebook. But the words 'Police', 'Crime', 'Investigation', 'Trial', kept forcing their way into his ears, and he finally gave up trying not to pay attention. With his elbows on the desk and his hands cupped under his chin, he listened to the teacher praising the efficiency of the police and going into detail about the new scientific methods of crime detection. Ray could hardly believe the bad luck of having this lesson at this time. He could feel the pulse in his temple beating fast as the teacher gave examples of how shreds of clothing or dirt under the fingernails had been enough to convict criminals.

Then, just before the lesson ended, one of the girls in the class asked a question that lifted Ray out of his gloom. 'But sir, I thought that out of all the crimes that were committed only about forty per cent of them were ever detected and then solved?'

The teacher was obviously put out after his glowing praise of the police and he immediately turned on the girl and said sneeringly, 'And where did you get that ridiculous figure?'

The girl looked down at the desk. Ray knew how sarcastic this teacher could be and he saw that the girl had decided not to say any more. But then somebody else said:

'Yes, I heard that too, sir.'

And immediately a couple of other people called out:

'That's right, sir.'

'I heard it on the radio . . .'

'Yes, it was on telly, sir . . .'

The teacher was obviously angry, but he worked hard at calming down. 'Well, it sounds highly unlikely to me. However, it will be one of the things that you can find out about as part of your homework.' He smiled at the class. 'You can also copy this essay down to be done by Monday.'

While he wrote down the title on the board, people in the class turned and smiled at one another, pleased at having annoyed him. He was so sarcastic and full of himself that they enjoyed any chance of upsetting him. Ray, however, was too wrapped up in his own thoughts to take part in the silent congratulations and pleasure. The figures that the girl had quoted had offered a gleam of hope – even if she was wrong and it was only fifty per cent of the crimes that remained unsolved, even if it was only forty per cent. Up to that moment the police had seemed to be infallible, and the reminder that they also failed – frequently – to catch people, gave him new encouragement. Suddenly he felt safer.

The lesson ended, and everyone hurried off to the changing-rooms for P.E. In his new, more hopeful frame of mind, Ray entered fully into the hard training session and enjoyed concentrating on the exercises.

Just like the morning, the time passed quickly because he was thinking only of the work and he was surprised when the whistle was blown and everyone trooped up from the field to shower and change. He even joined in the shouting and flicking of towels as people stepped out of the steamy shower-room.

Having finished dressing, they pressed together round the notice-board where the P.E. teacher was posting the teams for next Saturday's football games. Dave, at the front of the group, turned and called to Ray:

'You've made it – you're reserve!'

Since the beginning of the season Ray had been trying to get in the team, and this was the nearest he had got. He felt a stab of pleasure that at last he was in the side – even if it was only as reserve.

Dave fought his way out of the crowd towards Ray and shouted:

'Let's get out of here.'

They left the building and walked together across the playground towards the school gates. 'I told you it was only a matter of time,' Dave reminded him.

'Yeah.' Already the pleasure had faded and as the worries began to beat in him again, Ray could not put much enthusiasm into his response.

Dave noticed and said, 'Come on – better to be reserve than nothing. It must mean that he's thinking of giving you a place.'

'I know.'

'Well, cheer up then.'

Ray started to smile. After all, it would be good to get a chance to play alongside Dave, who was a natural footballer – it had been his ambition to do that for the last two years.

They turned out of the gates and Ray was about to make a real effort to show some pleasure, in order to satisfy his friend, when he saw the police car coming along the road. It started to signal a left-hand turn and slowed down. He watched it drive into the school gates and up to the main building.

'It's the Law,' he heard Dave say. 'I wonder what they want?'

Ray's heart began to race, and the pressure built up to a whistle in his ears. Trying to control himself, he joined Dave, who had turned and started to walk down the road. He could feel the panic threatening to overwhelm him, but rising above it came an even more powerful emotion – he had to know. He couldn't simply walk away from the school without knowing what was happening – he knew that the doubt would drive him mad. He had to know whether they had found out – he had to go back and see what they wanted, perhaps it was nothing to do with him.

He grabbed his friend's arm.

'I've forgotten something. I'll have to go back and get it.'

'What have you left?'

'Some money in my desk. I can't leave it.'

'O.K. I'll wait here for you.'

'No, it's O.K. – you go on.'

'I don't mind waiting.'

'No, really – don't. There's no point in hanging around.'

Dave hesitated and Ray prayed that he'd go.

'All right then. See you tomorrow.'

'Yes, see you.'

Ray turned and walked back towards the school. He was being stupid. He couldn't go barging in and ask the cops what they were doing there. He might even attract attention to himself if they merely saw him hanging around. It was worse than stupid – it was dangerous. Yet he had to go.

A few people glanced at him as he headed back through the school gates, but he ignored them and made an effort to pull himself together. By the time he'd reached the main door, the stream of people leaving had died down. He walked around to the side entrance that linked the old and new parts of the school, dropped his case and shoulder-bag containing his soccer kit and kicked them together against the wall. Then he opened the door and glanced around. The corridor was deserted. Looking once more over his shoulder to check that no one was watching, he slipped inside and closed the door quietly behind him.

He stood and listened. Somewhere above, a bucket rattled as the cleaners started clearing up the class-rooms. There was no sound from the far end of the corridor where the headmaster's office was. The police would be either in with the Head or in the secretary's office next door. He began to tiptoe in that direction.

He heard a door open and the secretary's voice echoed along to him: 'If you wait there, I'll see if he's free.'

Ray darted into one of the nearby class-rooms. He heard the secretary's footsteps, a knock, and then the sound of a door being opened and closed. He became aware of the loudness of his breathing and the knock of the blood pounding in his ears. He peered out, keeping his body hidden inside the room. The secretary emerged from the headmaster's office, stood outside her own, and beckoned. Two policemen followed her back towards the Head's room. He heard the door close, and the secretary walking back to her room. Good – she had closed her door, too.

He waited a moment, leant out and checked that there was nobody there, and then he started walking silently up towards the office. When he was nearly opposite the door, he stopped and faced the notice-board – if anybody came out, he could pretend that he was just reading the notices. He listened. Nothing – he couldn't even hear the sound of voices. He moved along to the very end of the board and listened again. There were still some distant bangs, and scraping sounds from upstairs where the cleaners were working, and now he could hear the click of the secretary's typewriter. But no voices.

He held his breath and began to step backwards towards the Head's door, still facing the direction of the notice-board, though by now he was too far away to convince anyone that he was really reading the notices.

He heard footsteps coming down the stairs, and he hastily made himself appear engrossed in the notice-board. Out of the corner of his eye he saw Mrs Benson, the biology teacher, come down the last step and walk across to the staff-room. As she opened the door, he heard the sound of talking. Then there was silence again. She hadn't even looked his way.

He began to edge towards the room in which the policemen were talking to the headmaster, straining to hear. Gradually he caught the sound of voices, but it was impossible to distinguish words. It was impossible and dangerous and the only way he would actually hear anything was to put his ear to the door. He walked up to the door. If he stood there with his hand raised, he could pretend that he was just about to knock. He leaned forward until he began to catch words: – 'people', 'discussion', 'understand' – it all sounded harmless – surely they weren't discussing an accident or a crime. But it was no good – he couldn't be sure.

Should he knock on the door and just walk in? No, that would be pointless. They'd simply stop talking, and he'd be ordered out – and besides, that would really draw attention to himself. He wondered for a moment if he would hear more if he went outside and tried to listen at the window, but that would be too dangerous, and if anyone saw him, it would be impossible to think of an excuse for being there.

He walked back towards the notice-board for safety and racked his brains. As he stood there thinking, he heard the door handle rattle and a voice say loudly, 'I'll just get the report from the car.'

The door closed and heavy footsteps sounded behind him. He turned his head slightly. One of the policemen was walking down the corridor. In less than a minute he was back carrying a clipboard under his arm. Ray gazed hard at the notice-board as the door was opened, and to add to the effect he raised his hand and touched a piece of paper with his finger as if he was reading a particular line intently. He heard the headmaster say two words and then be interrupted: 'Ah, here's the report. Thank you, Constable, you can wait outside.'

Ray's arm dropped to his side and he felt himself sway – he hadn't heard much but it was enough. The two words that the headmaster had spoken before he was interrupted were – 'Blackston Road'.

Even before he had time to think about what he had heard, the constable was standing by his side. He smiled at Ray.

'Trouble, son?'

'What?' His voice was croaky and he cleared his throat.

'Waiting for the Head?'

'Oh, no. I'm just looking to find out something.'

The policeman laughed. 'Thought you were waiting to get ticked off.'

'No!' Ray tried to get a chuckle into his voice, but it only croaked, and he coughed once more.

'Me – I was always in trouble at school. Right little tearaway. Half my teachers would drop dead if they knew I'd ended up as a copper. Most of them thought I'd be on the other side of the law.'

The constable grinned and pointed to his hair.

'I used to reckon it was because of my ginger hair. Stood out, you know.'

Too terrified to think of anything to say, Ray murmured politely.

'I'm sure it was that,' continued the man. 'I used to be the first one anyone ever thought of if something had happened. Cor, no end of trouble.'

Ray smiled weakly and said, 'I'd better go now.'

The policeman nodded and looked back towards a large anti-smoking poster. Ray slipped quickly past the constable and headed towards the exit. He felt very conscious of the way he was walking, and he wanted to turn round to see if the policeman was watching him, but he resisted the temptation and pushed open the door and went outside. Grabbing his two bags, he ran across the playground, out of the school gates, and along the road towards home.

Eight

As Ray went into his house, Derek called out above the noise of the TV in the front room: 'Mum?'

'No, it's me.'

He climbed the stairs heavily, still panting from the long run from school. He dropped the bags on the bedroom floor, locked the door, and collapsed on his bed and closed his eyes. For a while his mind clouded over, and he lay still, listening to the distant sound of the TV below.

When he allowed himself to think about what had happened, it was in a totally calm way. So the police had somehow linked the accident with the school. Well, there was still no way they could possibly link it with him. And he wasn't even sure they weren't simply making a check on all the schools in the area. How could they know that it had been a young person who had stolen the bike? They were only guessing, that was all. After all, they had to start somewhere. What was the term? Making 'routine inquiries'. That was it. And yet, something troubled him about how close they had got, even though they probably didn't realize it. Unless – and a chill gripped his shoulders and neck as it came to him – unless they had got hold of the fact that someone calling himself John Timpson had got on a bus near the scene of the accident and had given a false name and address, using a road that was near the school. Supposing they had put two and two together and had guessed that the person had named Barnford Road only because he went to school near there. It wouldn't be so difficult to reach that conclusion. And he cursed himself for not having chosen a road that could not have been connected with him in any way.

He continued to think logically and was surprised how coolly he was working things out. Even if they had managed to get that far – and he felt sure that they hadn't – but even if they had, what could they do next? There were five hundred boys at his school. They would never single out one out of five hundred – how could they? But supposing they called the bus-conductor in, and they held an identity parade. The skin on his neck crawled as he thought of the scene. Five hundred boys lined up on the playground, while the conductor walked along looking at each face carefully. And then when he reached him – the flash of recognition, and the finger raised to point him out and all the faces turned to watch.

He jumped up and shook the picture from his mind. If he kept playing this game of 'If, If, If' he'd send himself mad. He had been right first time, they were just making a routine investigation.

The storm in his mind settled, and he felt a sudden certainty that he was safe and would never be caught. All he had to do was go on living normally and wait. It would be difficult at times, and he was bound to get scared, but if he sweated it out for about a week, the whole thing would be forgotten and the police would move on to solving other crimes.

Again, a dark cloth settled over his brain and hid his fears from himself. He began to change out of his school clothes into his casual ones. He put on his dark green corduroy trousers and reminded himself to get his mother to sew his jeans that evening. Then he checked the pillow. It was dry now, and there was no sign of any blood.

He looked out of the window and saw that it was completely dark outside. He checked his watch – 5.30. He'd better get tidied up before his mother got home. He made his bed rapidly, pulling the sheets and blankets straight and punching the pillows into shape. Then he unlocked his door and went to the bathroom and ran a basinful of hot water. He pushed his sleeves up and splashed the water on to his face. It felt good, and as he dried his face he was more relaxed than at any time for the last twenty-four hours.

He went downstairs and into the front room. Derek was lying on his stomach on the floor, watching a cartoon on TV. Ray could remember when he had done exactly the same thing, and he became aware of his fondness for his brother. Derek could be an absolute nuisance at times, and they frequently quarrelled, but Ray could see himself in him. And yet in many ways he felt that he didn't really know him, that they were separate people. But you could look at him sometimes and see him thinking deeply, and you knew that he would only speak about it if he wanted to. There was a lot that he didn't say.

Ray wanted to get near him – to know his brother – but he didn't know where to begin. He tapped Derek's foot with his own and said: 'Did you have a good day at school?'

'Not bad,' Derek replied without turning round from the cartoon programme.

'What did you do?'

'The usual.'

'Do you like it there?'

'It's O.K.'

Stone-wall answers. It was obvious that he was going to give nothing away. Ray leaned back in the chair and watched the cartoon characters bashing hell out of one another. In a remote way, he thought of how easily the old lady had been destroyed by the motor-bike, and he wished human beings could bounce back to life like the animals in the cartoon.

'Hello, you two. I'm back,' their mother said, popping her head round the door.

Derek didn't turn round from the TV. 'Hi.'

'Hello, Mum.'

As his mother closed the door, Ray felt a sudden rush of feeling for her. He got up and followed her into the kitchen and helped her take off her coat. As she filled the kettle and put it on the gas-stove, Ray noticed that she was pale and her eyes rather red, as if she had been crying. He went up to her and with an aching need to get close to her, he stood in front of her and put his hands on her shoulders.

'What's up, Mum? Are you tired?'

She nodded and smiled weakly.

'A bit. Grandma isn't very well. I'm a bit worried about her and you know what a fusspot she can be.'

He looked directly at her. He was almost taller than her now, and he felt as though he could protect her – especially now when she looked so fragile.

'Cheer up,' he said. 'I'll make you a cup of tea.'

'That's my boyfriend.'

She managed a smile as she said it, but her eyes were strained with tension and worry. He wanted to pull her close and hug her as he had done when he was a kid, but he didn't. He started making the tea, and as he was getting the cups down, he heard her open the fridge door.

'Where have you put the sausages, dear?'

He knocked one of the cups over, and it rocked and rattled in the saucer.

'Oh, Mum . . .'

'What?'

'I forgot them.' He felt furious with himself – couldn't he do anything right?

'Oh, Ray – you promised. How could you forget? Now we've got nothing for tea, and the shops'll all be shut.'

Her face grew tighter and harder as her temper rose, and her eyes brimmed. Ray felt helpless and awkward – there was nothing he could do. 'I'm terribly sorry,' he mumbled.

'Well, that's not much use is it? We won't be able to eat your sorries. You really make me cross. I've had such a dreadful day and now you make it worse.'

She was almost crying now, and Ray felt a great gulp of air fill his lungs. He wanted to call out to her, to beg her forgiveness. He walked over to her to put his hands on her shoulders again and tell her how much he loved her and how sorry he was. But as he reached out his arms, she turned away. 'And don't think you can get round me like that.'

He felt stung. All the tension and agony of his day sprang out of him as he yelled at her:

'Oh, for crying out loud, don't go on. It's only a few silly sausages.'

'And don't you talk to me like that.'

'Oh, why don't you shut up?'

He caught a glimpse of his mother's hurt expression as she turned round to him, but nothing stopped him as he walked out of the kitchen, slammed the door, and stamped up the stairs. In spite of his hurt and anger, he already felt despair sweep over him. It had all gone wrong. He'd nearly been so close to her; then suddenly things had snapped and now they were so far apart.

He couldn't bear to think about anything, and he wished he could remove his memory from his brain. He put on the first record he could find and turned the volume up to nearly full. Then the music filled the room, but he felt wildly restless and started walking backwards and forwards. He looked aimlessly at his books, running his finger across them like a stick against a fence. He walked along the walls looking at the posters, photographs, wallpaper, anything he noticed. He began beating his fists on the wall in time with the music. As the guitars wailed and the drums pounded heavily, he beat harder on the walls. Gradually he increased the rhythm, drumming louder and louder, and hitting the wall so frantically that his whole hand ached. The music ended suddenly, and in one last surge of anger and despair he drove his knuckles savagely against the wall.

The pain shot through his body, and as it did he felt the pressure of his brain ebb away. He moved over and turned off the record-player, then looked at his hands. The knuckles were skinned, one or two of them bleeding slightly, and the sides were red and burning where he'd beaten them. He must be going mad – they'd be putting him in a strait-jacket soon. Fancy wandering round the room smashing up your hands. No doubt about it, it would be the funny farm for him. The words 'funny farm' struck him as hilarious, and he began to chuckle to himself. He sank on to the bed and lay back against the wall. 'Funny farm,' he said aloud and started to shake with laughter. The two words were so absurd and yet so cruel and bitter that he kept exploding into snorts of laughter. As his amusement died down, he lay full-stretch on the bed and closed his eyes.

All his agony was gone, and he felt relaxed and tired and distant. Even when he heard the door open and Derek's voice say, 'What have you done to Mum?' he just didn't care. He lay without answering, and Derek went away.

What have I done to Mum? Forgotten some stupid sausages, that's all, and if she wants to get upset about that, then it's her look-out. He felt cool and unexciteable as he thought about it. So he'd forgotten the sausages – O.K., it was a mistake and he was sorry, but there was no need for her to make such a fuss about it. After all, if she knew what had made him forget, she'd understand pretty quickly.

Somewhere at the back of his mind he knew that that was partly the reason that he had snapped – the fact that he couldn't tell her.

Later he heard his father come into the house. He sat up on the bed and waited, preparing himself for his father to come up and see him. He was bound to. It seemed ages, but at last he heard the footsteps on the stairs. There was a moment's pause before the knock on the door.

'Ray? Can I come in?'

Even in the worst moments, his father was always polite and considerate and made sure that Ray knew that his room was private and belonged to him. Still smarting, Ray found it very difficult to answer.

'Yes,' he called out awkwardly.

When his father came in, Ray saw that he hadn't changed

after work – something he normally did as soon as he got home. He glanced down and kept his eyes focused on the carpet as his father cleared his throat.

'What's happened?' he said quietly.

Ray wished his father would be less reasonable, that he would shout or hit him. When his dad spoke to him quietly like that, it always made Ray feel in the wrong.

After a long pause in which he hoped that he wouldn't have to speak, he finally said, 'Oh, I don't know. I forgot to get some flipping sausages and Mum did her nut. Blimey, I didn't mean to forget them.' He felt resentment build up again and mumbled, 'She's always going on at me.'

'Now come on, Ray, that's not fair. She's not always going on at you, and you know it.'

'Well, she flipping went on today.'

He felt his eyes begin to fill, and he clenched his jaw hard in order not to let the tears come.

His father sat down on the chair and sighed. 'Well, if she did, there was a good reason.'

'Just because I forgot some sausages?' he burst out.

'Now stay calm. No, not because you forgot the sausages. She's had a bad day at your grandma's. You know how close she is to her mother, don't you?'

Ray nodded and felt a tear drop on to his lap. He gulped and struggled not to let any more come.

'Well, Grandma's not very well. In fact she's very ill – she may well have to go into hospital for an operation. And your mum's worried about it, naturally, and she came home very upset. And then when she found out that you'd forgotten to buy the things for our tea, everything suddenly got on top of her, and she snapped at you. But you know she didn't really mean it, don't you?'

He nodded again and still stared hard at the carpet, tracing the pattern with his foot. It was so infuriating. When his father explained things in his calm way, it made you see why people behaved badly, and then you felt so rotten. But if he understood his mum, why couldn't he understand him? Surely if he told him now his father would understand how it had all happened, how things had just gone wrong. He started.

'Well, if you knew,' he blurted out, 'you'd see why I forgot.'

'Tell me, then.'

Yes, he would – he'd tell everything and get this terrible weight off him.

'Well, you see . . .' He looked up and straight into his father's eyes, and the steadiness and kindness there broke his resolution. He couldn't destroy what his father thought of him. The lie slipped easily off his tongue. 'Well, I found out that I've been picked for the football team on Saturday, and it just put it out of my mind.'

His father's face creased into a smile, and that was what Ray wanted – the pride and the pleasure. 'That's great. Oh, I am pleased – you've been waiting a long time for that.'

'It's only as reserve – but at least it means that Mr Raines thinks I'm nearly good enough to play.'

'Of course it does. I'm really pleased.'

His father stood up and came and ruffled his hair. 'Well, it's no wonder you forgot your errand. Anyway, let's forget all about that, eh? Your mum's cheered up, and we're going to have some eggs instead. It was all a fuss about nothing.'

He went to the door and opened it, then turned round and looked at Ray. 'Just say something to your mum, O.K.? It'll make her feel a lot better, and it'll clear the air for good.'

'O.K.'

'That's my boy. Tea'll be ready in a couple of minutes.'

He closed the door, and Ray wanted to howl after him, but he didn't. He wasn't his boy.

Nine

The tea went off easily with everybody laughing and joking about the sausages and saying how they all preferred eggs. His mother smiled and said, 'I'm sorry too', when he apologized, and then everybody congratulated him on being chosen for the team and laughed when Dad said, 'A couple of years and we'll all be living in luxury when you're playing for the City.' They ate and chatted, and the atmosphere was easy and light, and his father winked at him and nodded when he offered to do the washing-up. His mother started to object, but his father said, 'No, love, you go and sit down and have a bit of a rest. Ray and I'll do it, won't we, Ray?'

While Derek went upstairs to get ready for bed, his mother went into the front room. Ray washed up and his father dried and chatted about football and made him laugh about what had happened at work that day.

When they had finished, Ray tipped the bowl over and wiped the sink as the water drained away. His father hung up the tea-towel and said, 'I think I'll go and change and then watch the telly for a while. Anything good on tonight?'

Ray thought.

'Thursday? I don't know – there might be a film on.'

'Suits me – though I expect your Mum'll want to watch one of her flipping serials. Still, I feel in the mood to watch whatever rubbish is on. What about you?'

'I've got a bit of homework to do first.'

'O.K. – see you later, then.'

He followed his father upstairs and then went into his bedroom and closed the door. He sat on the edge of the bed and looked through his case for his books. There was some science to do, but it wasn't due for a couple of days, so he decided to leave it. There was the history essay too, but he couldn't risk the thoughts that it would bring back, so he'd leave that for a couple of days too. Instead, he got out his maths books and looked at the exercises that had to be finished for the next day. He put his exercise-book on the small table next to the bed and began working at the problems.

For about twenty minutes he worked steadily, then his concentration started slipping, and his mind wandered off a couple of times – always to the same terrifying fears that lay in his brain ready to bring a chill to his body whenever he thought of them. He got up and put a record on, though he had to keep the volume down because of Derek, who slept in the room next to his. He stood for a moment and combed his hair in front of the mirror before forcing himself back to the maths. By the time the L.P. finished, he was nearly through the last of the problems. He let the needle crackle and hiss in the groove for the minute that it took to underline the answer; then he lifted the arm and turned off the record-player. He closed the books and packed them back into the case, finished for the night.

He went downstairs and into the front room. His mum and dad were watching the TV and he sat down on the sofa and stretched his legs. It *was* one of the serials that his mother always watched, and after a minute he felt a kick on his foot. His father leant across and said in a mock whisper, 'It's nearly finished. It's been going on for hours. I think Mrs Boon will get a divorce and run off with the doctor – but he'll turn out to be a compulsive drinker and he'll throw her out of the window in a drunken rage!'

'Oh, shut up, Bob,' said his mother. 'You always try and spoil my programme.'

'Well, it's rubbish.'

'No, it's not, it's lovely. Anyway, if you don't like it I do, and you'll just have to put up with it, so there.'

Ray laughed and put his fingers to his lips. 'Ssh, you two – I'm trying to watch.'

His father threw a cushion at him and grinned.

Ray lay back on the sofa and closed his eyes. It was so cosy here watching the TV with his parents. He loved them both very much, and everything would be perfect if only ... He sat up and snapped his attention back to the TV – he was not going to let himself think about that.

The two people on the screen were holding each other and mumbling about how terrible it was to love like this – only seeing each other every month. Then the camera drew away from them and showed another man watching them from the doorway. The music swelled up and the credits began to roll across his face as he looked at them.

'Told you,' said his father. 'She'll leave him next episode.'

'No she won't. Now you can have your rotten old film.'

'At last! Turn it over, Ray.'

He got up and switched the set to another channel.

His mother groaned.

'Oh, not another war film! That's all we ever get on the telly. War, war, war. I'll go and make a coffee. Who wants one?'

'Yes, please, love.'

'No thanks, Mum. I think I'll go and have a bath. I'm a bit tired.'

'Right then.'

It was true actually – he did suddenly feel very tired. As he dragged himself upstairs he realized how much the day had taken out of him, and all he wanted to do was have a bath and crash into bed.

While he ran the water, he remembered his torn jeans. He picked them up and took them down to his mother. She was in the kitchen making the coffee and she jumped in surprise when he called to her. It was obvious that she was still feeling nervous, and her hands shook as she poured the water into the cups.

'Mum, I wondered if you could mend my jeans for me? I ripped a hole in the knee yesterday.'

She put down the kettle. 'Let me have a look at them.'

She examined the tear and pursed her lips. 'I'll never be able to sew that up without showing.'

'Why not put a patch on them?'

'Well, they'll look terribly scruffy.'

'That's all right – they look good with a patch at the knee, especially if it's a different colour.'

She laughed.

'Fancy wanting a patch that shows. All right – I'll see if I can find something in my work-basket. Leave it to me.'

He felt grateful that there had been no questions about how they'd been torn, and he was glad that all the trouble earlier had been forgotten. He squeezed her shoulder. 'Thanks, Mum. I don't know what I'd do without you.'

She looked at him and smiled. 'You'd manage! Now go and turn off the tap before you flood the whole bathroom.'

'Oh, I forgot!'

'It's that kind of a day,' she said and they both laughed.

Upstairs, he felt the water and then ran the cold tap while he got undressed. He put one leg on the edge of the tub and examined his knee – the bruising was fading, and a scab had formed over the graze. He tested the temperature again, then turned off the tap and got into the bath. It was just right. He lay back, keeping the grazed knee out of the water and watching the slight ripples rock against the little round island of dry flesh that it made. It was so relaxing lying there, though, that he finally decided that it wouldn't loosen the scab if it got wet and he straightened his leg and let it sink below the surface. He closed his eyes and the warmth seeped through his body.

He glanced at his watch, which was balanced on the edge of the towel-rail. 9.20. Twenty-six hours ago everything had been normal – he had had no problems. The heat from the water was beginning to sap his strength, and he recognized the growing gloom as his body and mind relaxed and lost their defences.

The Romans were supposed to have committed suicide in the bath. If the water was hot enough, it was apparently easy to cut your wrists without any pain. He pictured the water growing redder as his blood flowed from his veins, and he imagined the light growing dimmer as he slipped into unconsciousness. He looked up and saw his father's razor hanging next to the mirror above the sink. All he had to do was take out the blade, make two quick cuts, and all his problems would be solved. No more lies, no more fears. His parents would be upset, of course, but not as upset as they would be if they found out what he had done. It would be easier for them to face living without him than having to live with him if he was accused of killing someone.

Slowly he stood up and reached across. He unhooked the razor from the rack and twisted the handle. The top opened like a flower, revealing the blade lying inside. He slid it out with the tips of his fingers and put the empty case down on the edge of the sink, then sat down in the water. He held the blade out and looked at it – there was a film of soap and tiny pieces of bristle where his dad had forgotten to wash it thoroughly that morning, but one side was clean and sharp looking. Supposing it was blunt and wouldn't cut easily? He pictured himself having to hack and slash at the skin, and he remembered a film – a foreign film that he'd seen on TV – where a man had stuck the blade in some wood and then smashed his wrist down on to it. He shivered, his mind twisting and writhing away from the idea. He couldn't do it. He stood up abruptly, slopping water over the side of the bath, and hurriedly replaced the blade and hung the razor where it belonged.

Repulsed at the whole idea of what he had been considering, he grabbed the soap and flannel and scrubbed himself savagely, as though he could scrape the memory and his disgust from his body. He sank into the water and washed the soap off and then stood up and soaped and scrubbed himself again.

When he sat down again in the water he noticed that he'd knocked the scab off his knee and that a thin stream of blood was trickling into the water. And he knew that, whatever else happened, he would never again think about taking his life – it was stupid and impossible. Somehow he would get through it all and not let it break him. While he fought to drive his moment of stupidity out of his mind, he felt the strength and hope ignite inside him and the more determined he grew to carry on, the more sure he became that it would all work out. It would.

He dried himself briskly while the water drained down the plug-hole, and his skin tingled and glowed with life. He put on his pyjamas, brushed his teeth, and avoided looking at the razor hanging innocently beside the mirror. After sloshing some clean water round the bath, he hung up his towel and went downstairs and into the kitchen. What he needed was a good night's sleep and then he'd be able to face whatever the next day brought. He took three aspirins from the cupboard and gulped them down with a drink of water – just in case he found it hard to get to sleep.

He glanced into the front room. His father was still watching the telly, but his mother was sitting sewing his jeans. She held them up and pointed to the red patch that she was skilfully stitching into the hole at the knee.

'Bright enough for you?' she called.

'Perfect!'

His father turned and looked and made a joking sound of disgust. 'You going to bed then?'

'Yes – I'm really tired. 'Night.'

' 'Night, love.'

' 'Night, Ray.'

His bed was soft and cool. He wriggled into a comfortable position, feeling the dampness of his hair against his forehead. He yawned and sleep came quickly.

He woke once during the night and was aware of the shadow of a dream that he had just left – something sinister and frightening about rats darting out of dark corners at him. But he turned over and was asleep again even before he could really remember it.

Ten

He should have been rested after his heavy sleep, but as he woke up, he could feel a pain behind his eyes, and his mouth tasted foul. All his limbs ached, and his head felt heavy. He tried to get comfortable, but his bed-clothes were all rumpled and twisted – he must have been moving violently in his sleep. What day was it? Friday. He fumbled for his watch on the table – 7.30. He'd slept for nearly ten hours. He ought to be feeling good, but he wasn't. Friday – that meant that the local paper would be out. He had to get up and see if there was anything in it about the accident, more details than yesterday's daily. He sat up and his head throbbed with the effort, and he felt a vague sickness at the back of his throat. He pushed himself off the bed and stumbled to the door, his eyes half-closed.

In the bathroom he splashed water on his face to wake himself up, then peered in the mirror at his pale face. His tongue was coated thickly. He brushed his teeth and then gargled with water. As he leant backwards to let the water surge round the back of his mouth, another wave of sickness hit him. He spat and examined his tongue again. No change.

He walked out of the bathroom and back to his room, bumping against the door-frame as he went in. He collapsed on to the edge of the bed and held his head in his hands. He must be ill, he felt really terrible. He had to see the paper, though, and he stood up unsteadily and began to dress slowly. He brushed his hair and felt his legs trembling as he stood. He held tight to the banister as he walked downstairs and then pushed open the kitchen door.

The room was empty. His father's used plates were on the

table and the paper was propped up against the teapot. He sat down and began turning the pages back to the beginning – his father had left it folded on the sports page. It was the second biggest headline on the front page:

WOMAN DIES IN MYSTERY CRASH

Mrs Maureen Chalmers (63) was knocked over and killed on Wednesday evening as she stepped out of her car on a lonely road near her home in the village of Blackston. Her body was found next to an abandoned motor-bike which had been stolen earlier in the evening from outside the 'Green Man' on the Latchford Estate on the west side of the City.

NO PETROL

Mrs Chalmers, who was well-known in the district for her hospital work, left home at 7.50 and was discovered dead half an hour later by the side of her car. The Austin Mini she was driving was later found to be out of petrol.

PASSERS-BY

The body was first seen by Mr and Mrs Irwin who were driving from the village. They stopped and recognized Mrs Chalmers, then went back to Blackston and phoned for the police and an ambulance. Mr Irwin told our reporter that he thought the accident had only just happened when they stopped but that they had not seen any sign of the motor-bike rider.

TRAGEDY

Mrs Chalmers' husband has gone to stay with friends nearby, and a neighbour said, 'It's a tragedy. They were such a happy couple and were looking forward to Mr Chalmers' retirement next year.'

Det. Supt. Johnson said that the police were trying to trace the rider of the stolen bike.

He had known what he was going to read, and the article didn't tell him anything very new, but he felt dazed as he reached the end. It all looked so final and inescapable in the black and white of the newspaper.

The kitchen door clicked open, and his mother came in.

'Hello, Ray. Your breakfast is in the oven. It's egg and bacon. Your dad's gone already – he had to get off early today.'

He folded the paper quickly and put it down on the table as his mother passed him. She opened the oven door and started to take out a plate.

'I'm not hungry, Mum. I feel a bit sick.'

'All the more reason to eat your breakfast – it'll give you strength. It's just hunger sickness.' She put the plate in front of him, then turned back to the stove.

'Honestly I can't eat it,' he mumbled. The food glistened brightly.

'Nonsense. Eat it up. You'll feel much better.'

He lifted his knife and fork and held them poised over the plate. 'The police were trying to trace the rider of the stolen bike.' His stomach lurched. The fold in the paper allowed him to see just the last line of the article. He drew his knife across the top of the fried egg, and as the yolk began to slide out of the slit he had made, his stomach heaved. He dashed from the table and out of the room, up the stairs, and burst open the bathroom door.

'Hey, what are you . . .' Derek began as he rushed past, and then he backed out of the door as Ray leant over the lavatory and began to be sick.

He was gagging and still gripping the sides of the bowl when his mother said from the doorway, 'Are you all right, Ray?'

He coughed and wiped his mouth and managed to say, 'Yes. Leave me alone. I feel sick.'

He heard the door close and his mother talking to Derek. 'No, leave him alone. He'll be all right. Just get dressed and come downstairs.'

The wave of nausea passed, and he stood up, trembling, and pulled the chain. He rinsed his face in cold water and swirled water round his mouth. He felt drained and weak as he went to his room and lay down gently on the bed. He kicked off his shoes and pulled a blanket over himself. After a couple of minutes, his mother came in. 'Are you better, dear?'

He kept his eyes closed and grunted, 'Yes.'

'Can I get you anything? A drink?'

'No thanks.'

'Well look, slip your clothes off and get into bed properly. You obviously can't go to school like this.'

'O.K.,' he mumbled.

'Try and get some sleep.'

He nodded and heard the door close. He sat up slowly and pulled off his shirt, then stood up, undid his trousers and let them drop, then fell back on to the bed. His teeth started to chatter from the cold, so he pulled the covers over himself. He began to doze as his body warmed up the bed.

Some time later he felt his mother shaking his shoulder gently. 'Ray.'

He opened his eyes and rolled over on his back.

'How are you now?'

'A bit better, I think.'

'Good. You still look a bit pale, so I think you ought to stay in bed. Do you want anything to drink or do you still feel sick?'

'No, I feel a bit queasy.'

'Right. Now listen, Ray. I've just got to go over and see Grandma – the doctor's coming today, and I really must be there to see what he says. Do you think you'll be all right if I leave you?'

'Yes, that's fine. I don't think I'll be sick again.'

She bent down and felt his forehead, brushing his hair aside.

'I don't think you've got a temperature,' she said, testing her own forehead and then laying her hand across his again. 'No – it feels normal.'

He felt wide awake now, and he raised himself up on his elbows. 'I'll be fine, honest. I'll just lie here for a bit and then get up later.'

'Good – but don't get up unless you really feel like it. I don't know what time I'll be back, but it probably won't be until mid-afternoon.'

'O.K.'

'I'll see you later then. Take care of yourself.'

'Yes. 'Bye.'

She went, and Ray lay down again. A couple of minutes later he heard the front door slam, and he then listened to the silence of the house. Outside it was bright, and a thin November sun was shining into the room. The muscles of his stomach ached, and he rubbed them gently. He didn't feel sleepy any more. He lay on his side with one arm propping him up and read a football magazine from cover to cover even though he'd read most of it before.

When he finished it, he decided he would get up. He dressed slowly and washed himself again. He certainly looked better now – his face had been almost green earlier. Downstairs he put the kettle on and switched on the radio. He made a pot of tea and put it on a tray with a bottle of milk, the sugar and a mug and carried it into the front room. He went back into the kitchen and switched off the radio just as a stupid D.J. was gabbling through some request from a housewife. He picked up the local paper and went and sat on the sofa in the front room. It was cold in there so he switched on the electric fire and poured himself a cup of tea.

He read the story about the accident three times and examined each sentence carefully – there was definitely no suggestion that anything had been found out about him, and even the sentence about the inquiries about the rider of the bike no longer filled him with dread. They could make inquiries until they burst. There was nothing to connect him with it.

He drank another cup of tea and read through the rest of the paper. It was a real rag – there was no proper news, just reports about people being fined for speeding and parking, and stories about jumble-sales and minor fires in houses. It seemed to dig desperately for news and he imagined the big splash it would make if he was ever found out. It would be on the front page and all the gossips would have a field-day reading it and talking about it.

He threw the paper down and stared across the room. He felt sorry for all the people whose names had been put in that paper for doing wrong things. One man had been found drunk at a railway-station, and they had printed his name and address, as they had with a woman who had stolen a dress worth £14. People all over the city and the area could read about these people and in some strange way get pleasure from their unhappiness. It made him angry. He had never thought about it before, but the danger of his position made him sympathize with other people in trouble.

He stared at nothing. It was ridiculous that he even cared about anything like that when he was in so much trouble himself but he did. He would not get caught. He would *not* let all the nosey people have the pleasure of talking about him and coming to his parents to say how sorry they were.

Ideas began to flash into his mind. How could he put the police off the scent? How could he stop them getting any closer than they were? Perhaps even sending them off in the wrong direction? If he could only hold out for a couple of months, they'd stop making inquiries, and he'd be safe. He thought of mystery films he had seen and books he had read, but they were all too impossible – *he* couldn't leave the country and hide in South America. Supposing he wrote a letter confessing to the killing and posted it from another town? His mind played over the possibility. He would have to disguise his writing – use printing or even type it. He could cut out letters from a newspaper and stick them together to make the words, like in a ransom note. That was safer than writing or typing, both of which could be traced. Then there was the problem of posting it from another part of the country, the farther away the better. London would do. But how could he get it down to there and then get it posted back?

His mind wandered off on to what he would actually say. Phrases like 'I did it,' popped into his head. 'I killed the old lady near Blackston. It was an accident and I have decided to end my own life to pay for my crime.' That would be good if he could make them believe that the person responsible was dead.

But how to post the letter? Perhaps go down to London himself? He could just about raise the money, and it was possible to get there and back in a day. But it would be difficult to explain to his parents where he was going – it would take a whole day and it would involve more and more lies. Perhaps he could send the letter to someone and ask him to post it for him. He had some relatives in London and then there was his friend Chris, who had moved down to the South Coast a couple of years ago. No, that was no good – they'd see the envelope addressed to the police, and they'd be bound to ask what was happening. He'd have to post it himself. If needs be he'd have to choose some nearer place, which he could get to and back quickly, before he was missed.

He worked at the contents of the letter again: 'I killed Mrs Chalmers. I couldn't help it, and now I'm going to kill myself. I'm sorry for what I did, and this is the only way out.' It sounded corny – the police would never be fooled by a letter like that, or would they? The arguments for and against tumbled round his brain until he could no longer judge whether it would work or not. But at least he was now doing something to get himself out of the mess. Up to this moment he had been whirled round and round by events, and everything had happened *to* him. Not any more. In future he was going to make things happen for him – he was going to turn the wheel.

He glanced at his watch – quarter to one. He felt stronger now and charged with the positive thinking he had done. He no longer felt helpless – he must hope and *do* things. First, he had to stop acting in a way that brought attention to himself. If he hurried, he could get into school, say that he'd been a bit ill, and then get on with things as though he didn't have a worry in the world.

He went into the kitchen and made himself a cheese sandwich. He still didn't feel very hungry but he knew that he had to eat to stay fit and alert. While he ate the sandwich, he scribbled a note for his Mum, casual and reassuring:

'Feel much better so I've decided to go back to school. Hope Grandma is O.K. Love, Ray.'

Quickly he got his school things together and put on a jacket and tie. There would probably be a training session after school, so he grabbed his soccer things too, then left the house.

The day matched his optimistic mood – the mist which had partly veiled the sun had disappeared, and now the sun shone down from a deep blue sky like a spring day. He took a deep breath and caught the sweet smell of fallen leaves and the freshness of the air. It was good to be alive, and he swung his duffle-bag in a burst of happiness.

Eleven

'What happened to you?' Dave asked as they walked along the corridor between the first and second lessons of the afternoon. 'I thought you must be ill, and I panicked in case you wouldn't be able to play tomorrow.' Ray had arrived just as school restarted and hadn't a chance to talk to anyone before this moment.

'Oh, I was sick this morning, but I'm miles better now. I'll be O.K. for tomorrow.'

'You'd better be.'

'I'm only reserve, remember.'

'I know, but I bet he gives you at least half an hour as substitute. He always does – then you can show him how good you are.'

'Some hopes!'

'Yes, you are – and you've got to convince yourself you are before you'll be able to convince him.'

They turned into the class-room. Their English teacher wasn't there yet so they sat side by side on the radiator.

'Did I miss anything this morning?' Ray asked.

'No, not much – we went through those maths questions. Then we had double geography – don't ask me what we did, I was half asleep. It was a drag, all about weather and stuff.'

'Anything else?'

'No. Oh, yes – a bit of drama in Assembly. Some school governor's wife was killed in a crash the other day, and we had big prayers and a minute's silence for her.'

Ray's heart jerked, and he must have sounded strange as he asked, 'What was her name?'

'Dunno, can't remember.' Dave called over to a group of girls who were sitting on the desks near the front chatting. 'Hey, Helen, what was the name of that governor's biddy who got killed?'

Helen looked up. 'Fancy calling her a biddy, poor thing.' She paused and frowned, trying to remember. 'I don't know — it was that lady on the front page of the *Courier*.'

'Oh, never mind. Thanks, anyway,' called Dave. He turned to Ray. 'In any case, they made a big fuss about her, and went on about how tragic it was and what a good bloke her husband was and how much he'd done for the school. Made a change from the usual stuff about pollution. Hey, watch it, here he comes!'

The English teacher came into the room, and everyone settled into his desk as the lesson began. But Ray wasn't listening. His heart pounded with excitement and relief. So that was it. Mr Chalmers was a governor of the school. The police hadn't come to see the headmaster yesterday about the possibility of the culprit being one of the pupils at the school. They had come to tell him that one of the school governors had lost his wife in a crash! They weren't near to finding out about him at all — it was just a fluke. Everything was going to work out fine. There were no problems — he wasn't going to be caught. After all his fears and worries! Ray felt terrific. He was going to get away with it. He felt a smile break out on his face with the sheer joy of it and ducked his head. He was still smiling even when he heard the teacher say, 'Ray, do you think you could possibly pay attention.'

'I was,' he said, looking up, and then added, 'What?'

The class laughed, and Ray sat beaming in confusion.

'I asked you to read three times.'

'Oh, sorry. Read what?'

The class laughed again as the teacher groaned and said, 'I give up. Sally, go on.'

Ray opened his book and looked at Dave's to see which page

they were on. He began to follow the story, but he felt like singing.

The double lesson flashed past, and Ray was still elated when the last bell of the afternoon rang. He joined Dave in the corridor, and they headed for the changing-rooms.

'Are you going to tell him that you were ill this morning or are you going to risk training?' Dave asked.

'Tell him? You must be kidding! I'm not going to give him the slightest chance of changing his mind about me now. Besides I feel great – it was only a bit of an upset stomach. I'm full of energy.'

'O.K., take it easy.'

'Blimey, you make me sound like an invalid.'

'No, I don't mean that – I just mean ... Oh I dunno, I'm just nervous. I really am. I wanted you to get a chance and now you have I don't want you to blow it.'

'Don't worry,' said Ray, smiling. 'I won't.'

'Well, where did all this confidence come from? Yesterday, you were determined that you'd never make the team.'

'I don't know. I just feel sure that everything will be O.K. – that's all. Anyway,' he added, 'thanks for caring.'

'Oh, shut up!'

'Charming!' laughed Ray and gave his friend a powerful nudge with his shoulder.

'Watch it, Superstar.'

They joined the others, changed quickly into their kit, and then ran out on to the field and began kicking a couple of balls around while they waited for the practice to begin. On this last session before the game, only the twelve who were actually named turned up, and it excited Ray to stand with the selected group. But he also felt rather distant from the others. They had all played together before, and he was the new boy. He grew more determined to do well.

When Mr Raines, the P.E. teacher who coached the Under 16's arrived, the session started. First, they did limbering exercises to warm themselves up. Then came the hardest part – fifteen minutes of non-stop sprint and trot, which left all of them panting and holding their sides.

Ray's illness that morning seemed to make little difference to him – he felt that he was almost less exhausted than anyone else. With nearly anybody else, Ray would have tried to prove this to the trainer by showing off a bit, but Mr Raines seemed to have an instinct for people who were trying to catch his attention, and he didn't like them. He was a great one for team effort, and although he recognized and appreciated individual skill he was wary of players who looked as if they might be more concerned with themselves than with the team. He was always saying, 'I want a skilful *team*, not eleven skilful players who can't play together.'

So Ray stood and panted and rested with the others – and he was grateful that he had to check his desire to show off, because it was something that he disliked about himself. It was strange – part of him wanted to shine at things and be better at them than others, and part of him was nervous and unsure of himself. Mr Raines seemed to be able to keep the show-off in him at bay and yet eliminate the nervousness at the same time. Ray didn't actually *like* him – he was a man who was too distant for that – but he did respect him and he knew that Raines brought out the best in him. He had that effect on everybody – the whole team wanted to succeed not for themselves but because Mr Raines somehow managed to make the team's success important.

When they had recovered their breath, they did some ball-control exercises and then a quarter of an hour's passing practice.

'That'll do for now. Go and change, and I'll be up in about ten minutes to have a quick word.'

They showered, dried themselves, and were starting to dress when Mr Raines came in. 'Just a couple of things,' he said. 'First of all, please make sure that your kit is clean for tomorrow. It'll probably mean nagging someone at home to wash and iron your things this evening but I expect your mothers are used to that by now. Secondly, make sure that you get an early night tonight. Be on time tomorrow. We've got a mini-bus arriving here at nine o'clock, and we must leave straight away, or we'll never get over to the ground in time. We've been doing well this season, and I think we stand a really good chance tomorrow. So I'll see you all in the morning.'

He came over to Ray and said quietly, 'Now, Ray, the team tomorrow is twelve strong. Do you understand? As our reserve, you are as important as anybody else who's on the field. I can't promise anything, but I'll try and see that you'll get some action. But whatever happens – you are part of the team, O.K.?'

Glowing with pleasure, Ray nodded and then bent down to put on his shoes to cover the idiotic expression he felt on his face. The training and hard work were suddenly rewarded. When he finished dressing he sat on the bench and waited for Dave and then both of them left and called out 'Good-bye' to the others.

'What did he say to you?' asked Dave as they left the school grounds.

'Oh, not much – just that he couldn't promise I'd play, but that he'd see how things were going.'

'Great. That means you'll play.'

'Don't be too sure.'

'Wanna bet?'

It was dark by the time Ray got home. He had forgotten his front-door key and had to ring the bell. Derek opened the door and then ran back into the front room without saying anything. Ray followed him and found him already sprawled out on the floor, watching TV.

'Is Mum back yet?'

'In the kitchen,' said Derek, eyes glued to the screen.

'You'll need glasses before you're ten if you sit that close.' Derek ignored him, and Ray walked out and into the kitchen.

His mother, who was peeling potatoes, turned and smiled at him.

'Hello, Mum. How's Grandma?'

Her smile faded, and she stopped her work and dried her hands on her apron. 'I'm afraid she's not too good. The doctor said she'll have to go into hospital for a check-up.'

'What did he say was up with her?'

She paused and sat down at the table. 'Well, he didn't say anything to her – just that she needed some rest. But afterwards I went to the door with him, and he said that he couldn't be sure but that it looked pretty serious. He said they'd have to do some tests, and then he'd be able to let us know some more. I don't know – I'm a bit scared by it all. She's getting on now, and I don't think she would be able to stand an operation.' She stopped and looked directly at Ray. 'You mustn't say anything to Derek – I don't want him worried.'

'Of course not.' He suddenly realized that his mother had been talking to him as she would to another adult, and he was glad. 'Anyway, don't worry, Mum, I'm sure she'll be O.K.' He smiled at the thought of his grandmother. 'She's really tough for her age.'

'I know, but she doesn't look well. I think she's probably lost a lot of weight.' She sighed and got up and started the potatoes again.

'Mum, I've got to get my football things washed for to-morrow –'

'Well, if you leave them down here, I'll do them after tea.'

'No, it's all right. I was going to say I'll do them. You've got enough to do.'

'Would you? I am a bit behind with everything – I didn't get back till late.' She turned and looked at him. 'Thanks, Ray. I appreciate it.'

He shrugged his shoulders. 'It's nothing. I'll do them up-stairs in the sink.' He walked to her side and picked up the soap-powder.

She shook the water off her hand and put her arm round

him affectionately. 'I mean it. Thanks.' As he climbed the stairs his eyes were watering, and he gulped with emotion. He loved her so much and when he did something that pleased her, his head buzzed with happiness. He wanted to be a good son and repay all the love he had been given. It haunted him in a way and he usually felt that he had turned out somehow not as good as he wanted to be. So when he did do something right, it choked him with joy.

He dumped his shirt and shorts into the wash-basin, ran the water, and added the soap-powder. He looked at himself in the mirror and noticed the shine in his eyes where he had almost cried. That was something else – he had to get out of this habit of seeing himself doing things. It was something that seemed to occur frequently now – it was almost as if he observed himself nowadays when anything happened. Not that he didn't really feel the things, but that he always caught himself watching himself being sad or happy or whatever it was – as if he were both the actor *and* the audience.

Besides he didn't have much right to feel that he was the dutiful son. What was doing his mother a small favour by washing his own clothes compared with the misery he would cause her if she learned the truth about him? But even as he thought it, he didn't really believe that she would ever have to know. The events of the day had given him confidence – he felt that after all his bad luck he was now due for some good, and that it had already started. He wasn't going to be caught, his parents were never going to know – he could be the model son. At least on the outside; if only it could be for real.

He pounded the clothes in the sink and created so many suds that he had to scoop some of the foam off the top and drop it into the bath. By the time he had washed and rinsed his clothes and then wrung them out it was nearly time to eat and his father had already come in from work and called out, 'Hello, everybody!'

Ray went downstairs and into the kitchen. 'Hiya, Dad. Hey, Mum, do you reckon these are as dry as I'll get them?'

His mother felt the clothes and said, 'We can squeeze some more water out, I think. Grab hold of this end and twist.' They held the clothes over the sink and managed to get some more water out.

'Now go and hang them over the tank in the airing-cupboard, to dry a bit more, and I'll iron them after we've eaten. Hurry up, though, I'm just going to put the food on the table. And drag Derek away from that blessed TV on your way back. Honestly, he does nothing else nowadays except watch that wretched thing.'

Ray dashed upstairs, hung the shirt over the tank, and then called to Derek on his way down, 'Come on, square-eyes, your tea's ready.'

They sat down and started to eat. 'Derek, don't gobble your food,' said his father.

'Oh, Dad, I want to watch the film – it's a cowboy.'

'I don't care. You'll make yourself ill if you gulp your food down like that.'

His mother's knife and fork clattered on to her plate, and Ray looked up quickly. 'Ray – I forgot all about it. Are you better?'

He released his breath – he had been suddenly frightened about what she was going to say. 'Oh, yes, I forgot, too. I'm fine. I feel terrific.'

'Why, what was the matter?' his father asked.

'Oh, it was nothing – I just felt a bit ill this morning, that's all.'

'Yes, it was horrible,' Derek started. 'He was sick all over the place.'

'I was not.'

'Yes, you were. I was in the bathroom, and you came in and started being sick everywhere . . .'

'That's enough, Derek,' interrupted his mother. 'We can do without the details while we're eating, thank you very much.'

'It was nerves about the match tomorrow probably. Did you do any training this afternoon?' His father was pointedly changing the subject.

Ray was only too pleased to skip over what had happened that morning, so they talked about the training and the match while they finished eating.

Again Ray volunteered to do the washing-up when the meal ended, and he worked in silence while his mother ironed the shorts and shirt. He finished clearing up and sat down at the table and watched while his mother folded and pressed his strip.

'There you are,' she said. 'What about your socks – do they need doing?'

'No, it's O.K. – I'll use my spare pair.'

'Right, I'm going to sit down and have a rest. I think you'd better put these in the cupboard again to make sure they air.'

He took his things upstairs and put them on the shelf just over the tank, then went into his room to get out his socks for the morning. He still felt happy and at his ease, but there was something stirring in him even as he bent down and pulled open the bottom drawer of the wardrobe. He pushed aside the sweaters to take out his socks and then as he did so he saw the parka.

He thought of the rip on the shoulder and of the blood-stains inside the hood, and he took it out to look at it. The tear really was very small, and when he searched the inside of the hood, he could barely see the smudges of dried blood.

Not knowing why, he put the parka on – zipped it up and pulled the hood up over his head. He turned round and saw his distorted image in the window. As he took the parka off again, he felt the first twinge of what grew into an irresistible desire. He was going to put on a thick sweater and take his scarf, and he was going out to Blackston Road.

Twelve

He jerked his push-bike out of the coal-shed and wheeled it into the street. He got on it and started pedalling towards the main road. After all, it wasn't as if he was going to steal a motor-bike. He was just going for a ride on his own bike, that was all. And he had told his parents this time – they had seen nothing odd when he had told them that he felt a bit restless and that he wanted some air and so he was going out for a ride on his bike. His father had merely said, 'Check your lights', and he had, so there was nothing wrong about what he was doing. Besides, it was true – he *was* restless and it would probably do him good to get a bit more exercise before the game – it would relax him.

At the main road, he turned left out into the bright lights, but even though he knew that he was heading in that direction, he still wouldn't admit to himself that he was going back *there*. There was a slight mist again – as there had been two nights ago, although it wasn't quite as cold as it had been then. Perhaps it was because he wasn't going so fast. He had really sped along this road before, and it had been easy, no effort at all, whereas now ... He crouched down and pumped the pedals hard, and the exercise made him warm.

It was ridiculous and crazy doing this. Doing what? He was simply out for a bike-ride. He would turn back in a minute and go home. It was dangerous, too – the police or someone might be hanging around there and see him. So what? He was an innocent bloke riding his bike along a road – nobody could think there was anything suspicious about that. Besides, he wasn't going there – he was just going to cycle up to the Angel Roundabout and then back again.

Cars whizzed past him, and he drew further into the side and concentrated on keeping as straight a line as possible and a steady speed. He gripped the handle-bars tightly and suddenly had a fear of wobbling slightly and being hit by a passing vehicle. Now that would be really funny – to end up like . . .

The roundabout was ahead. As he came up to it, he slowed and waited for a couple of cars that were going round it, then he drew out and hugged the middle. He would stay on the inside, go right round, and then back along the road he had just come on. He was still telling himself that when he stuck his left hand out and drew across towards the Blackston Road. It would be O.K. – he'd just cycle along past the place where it had happened and then go home.

The noise from the traffic ceased, and his light shook and wobbled, illuminating only a small part of the dark road ahead. There was no moon and only the thin beam of his headlight to see by. He could hear the tyres spinning along the tarmac. It was lonely. He had rounded the bend away from the glow of the main road and into the blackness of that long, long straight.

Why? This was so stupid. He had been warm and safe at home, and he could have stayed there and had a good evening. But that was the point – he couldn't. From the moment it had gripped him, he had known that the desire to come back here was irresistible. He had been drawn back – and there was nothing he could do about it. Yet only this morning he had been telling himself that he was the one in charge – that he was going to control what happened. Perhaps he was – *sometimes*.

He almost laughed out loud when the thought struck, but it also froze his bones. Could it be true? Surely not. And yet he had read it and heard it so many times in detective stories: a murderer always goes back to the scene of his crime.

He felt his scalp bristle at the thought – that was exactly what he was doing, and if he was doing it and if it was true, perhaps the police were expecting it to happen and were up there in the dark waiting for him. It wouldn't be a question of an innocent passer-by then.

He stopped the bike and turned off the light. He stood and strained his eyes and his ears. Was there anybody up there? It could only be a couple of hundred yards away now. If there was somebody there, he would have seen Ray's light coming and have seen it being switched off. Already he would be thinking that Ray was acting in a suspicious manner. Ray felt the sweat break out on his forehead and another trickle ran from his armpit down his side.

He peered into the blackness, waiting for a tell-tale sound, a cough, or a footstep crunching on the road as a policeman waited patiently for the killer to come back.

Nothing.

There was no sound, except far away the drone of traffic from the main road. He waited. Still there was no movement, no footstep, no cough and now he knew that he had to go on – that having got this far, he couldn't possibly turn back now. It was almost like a game, a dare – he had to push himself into the danger, into the trap. He got off his bike and wheeled it along, walking absurdly on tiptoe. He was wearing plimsolls – but even they seemed to make so much noise no matter how softly he stepped.

What would he say if there was somebody there? How could he explain away his strange behaviour? His mind raced to explanations and alibis, lies that would sound plausible. He had got off his bike because he felt sick, he would say – he had been sick that morning, they could check with his mother if they didn't believe him. What was he doing out riding at this time of night? He was training for a football game he was playing the following day – he was training hard because he was only a reserve for the game, and if he was chosen to play, he wanted to make sure he would do well. Why had he picked this dark, lonely road? Well, he had been cycling along the main road, and the fumes of the cars had made him feel sick, and he thought it would be better along a country road, but he had still felt sick and so he had had to stop and get off and . . . The circle was complete and his mastery of lying filled him with self-hatred.

He was almost level with it when he saw it – a dark object at the side of the road. It was square and stood about three feet tall. He turned the wheel towards the shape and switched on his front light.

It was a signboard. In paint it said:

POLICE NOTICE. APPEAL FOR WITNESSES.

Below that was some writing in chalk: 'Did you see an accident at this spot on Wednesday 26th November between 8.10 p.m. and 8.20 p.m.? An elderly woman in a maroon Austin Mini was knocked over and killed by a motor-bike.' Then in paint again:

ANY INFORMATION: RING 27/8603.

He read the notice, feeling absolutely nothing. His panic had gone, leaving him drained. He turned the handle of the bike and walked on. About twenty yards past the board, he stopped and shone the light across the road. This was where it had happened. There was no sign of it at all – no tyre-marks or glass or blood, yet he knew for sure that this was where it was. The Mini had stopped there. Mrs Chalmers had sat there inside her car. She had probably tried to start it again – but it was no good, her petrol tank was empty. She had turned off the ignition, wondering what to do. Should she walk back to the village or should she wait for a friendly motorist to stop and give her a lift? She would wait.

She had sat there, and the minutes had passed, and then she had probably seen the lights of his bike in the mirror. Someone was coming – someone who would take her home or, even better perhaps, someone who would take her to the garage and then bring her back with a can of petrol. As his lights had grown brighter she would have been filled with hope. She would have reached for the door handle, pressed it down. The door would have begun to open, the inside light would have snapped on. She would have slid out of the seat on to the road to stop this kind stranger. She would have heard the screech of brakes, seen the lights wobble, seen the bike hit and slide towards her. And then . . . nothing.

It was the first time that he had thought about Mrs Chalmers, had tried to see it from her point of view. Up to this moment he had been too wrapped up in his own fears and worries even to consider her, and yet she had played such an enormous part in it all. But now he had relived it through her eyes. He began to picture what he had done afterwards. He had run away, come back, rubbed off his finger-prints, dropped his scarf, run off into those trees over there . . . Yet that was not important – he knew all that well enough, he had lived through it. What mattered, and what kept coming to him as he stood there, was her part in it all – all the things she had done, all the thoughts she might have had, until the moment when she had ceased to think.

Then he saw them together – because that was it. It wasn't just her, and it wasn't just him – it had been both of them. From the moment he had left home that night, perhaps even before that – but he couldn't think about that now; from the moment he had left home, he and Mrs Chalmers had been heading towards each other. They had met briefly, had spoken, and had not seen the significance of it. They had met, then separated and gone their own ways for about ten minutes more, before they had reached the moment that he had just relived – the moment of collision.

He found himself standing on an empty, dark road thinking of nothing.

A wind stirred the tops of the trees nearby and he was alive again. There was a prickling at the side of his face as he once more became aware of the possibility of hidden eyes watching him, of the thought of being caught.

He leapt on the bike, jerked it round to the direction of home, and began pedalling furiously down the road; the vision was gone, and he was conscious only of his body pounding out the rhythm that took him away from that place of darkness and thoughts back into the world of light and movement.

Thirteen

He arrived home panting violently and sweating despite the cold of the night air. He had raced back over the entire journey, concentrating his whole mind and effort on pushing the bike as fast as it would go. His arms trembled with exhaustion as he manoeuvred the machine back into the shed, and the back wheel caught on something. He jerked it past the obstruction, and as he did so, one of the pedals ripped open a bag of sand. He quickly tapped the hole with his foot and prevented as much spilling as he could.

He went into the house by the kitchen door and gulped down two cups of water, then leaned against the sink to get his breath back. It was just half-past nine – it had taken nearly two hours to cycle there and back. All he felt like doing was washing and going to bed, but he'd been out for longer than he'd intended, and he really ought to spend some time with his parents. He drank another cup of water, wiped his face quickly on a towel, then went into the front room.

The TV was on, though neither his father nor his mother seemed to be watching it.

'Hello, Ray – you've been a long time,' said his father, putting the paper on the floor. It was the *Courier*, and Ray could see the headline about the accident and quickly wondered whether his dad had read it.

'Yes, I sort of got carried away and just went on riding. It was good exercise.'

His mother glanced up from her knitting and tutted. 'Oh Ray, your hair's soaking. You'll catch your death. Why don't you go and dry it.'

'No, it's O.K. – it's warm in here.' He sat down on the arm of the sofa and glanced at the TV, then down at the paper near his father's foot. He dared himself to say something about the accident – something like, 'Did you read about that poor old lady who got knocked over. She was the wife of one of the governors at school.' His mother was bound to have read it, and it would be interesting to hear them discussing it. The dare grew in his mind, a sort of stupid challenge to himself, but he shrugged it off. There was no point in drawing attention to it, he'd probably just end up frightened or depressed.

Even as he decided not to say anything, he caught his brain saying, 'You should have done it. It will be bad luck if you don't.' Immediately he retorted, 'Oh, no, you don't, the game's cancelled, it doesn't mean anything, it won't be bad luck.' It was amazing, he so often found himself playing this stupid 'dares and consequences' game with himself – almost as though part of him wanted to put a curse on the other part. It would all whizz through his mind in a second but it seemed as though he was determined to unnerve himself – to wish disaster on himself.

'I'm afraid I won't be able to come and watch the game to-morrow, Ray.'

'Oh, why not?'

'Grandma's got to go into hospital tomorrow morning, and Mum and I are going over in the car to take her. It'll be easier for her like that – better than going in an ambulance.'

Ray groaned slightly. He'd wanted his father to come and see him play, even though he'd been rather nervous at the thought of playing in front of someone he knew.

'It can't be helped, Ray. I was really looking forward to it.'

'Never mind – I may not play, anyway.'

'I'll definitely come next time.'

'Yeah. Is Derek going with you?'

His mother turned. 'No, he's going over to stay with Mrs Walker. There's no point in taking him – it'll only worry him.'

'I think you ought to tell him – I'd have been fed up if you hadn't told me.'

'Yes, but you're much older than he is. You can understand things that he can't.'

'I agree with you, Ray,' said his father, picking up the paper again. 'But we've talked it over, and your mum's made up her mind.'

'He's bound to find out eventually, Mum.'

'Well, perhaps he is, but she may be out in a couple of days, and then he won't ever have to know. Let's hope so, anyway.'

'I still think it's wrong. I think you ought to tell children things like that. If nobody says anything to you, it makes things all sort of secret and worse somehow. What are you going to tell him if she dies?'

'Oh, Ray, don't say things like that.'

'Well, supposing she does? I mean, she could. You'd have to tell him then.'

His mother looked up at him with an angry frown on her face. 'Now just stop saying things like that. There's no need to talk about it – it only makes things worse.'

Ray was going to add something, but he stopped himself. She was just on the point where a row could develop if he didn't shut up. He'd noticed before the way she seemed to run away from trouble – if you don't say anything, it might go away. Bit like an ostrich. But this was the first time that he'd ever been able to see it so clearly. And his father was a bit soft too – if he thought Derek ought to know, then he should tell him, instead of ducking out of it by giving in to her. It was done so as not to upset her, Ray knew, but it still seemed a bit weak. Everybody seemed to tread warily and make sure that she wasn't upset – even when they knew that what they were doing was wrong. In a way, that was part of why he couldn't mention what he had done. He felt a little bubble of hatred inside him against her. It was her fault.

He watched her knitting again and occasionally looking up at the TV screen, and the bubble burst, and the hatred drained away and he felt unkind and unfair in trying to blame her. How did these rotten feelings ever get inside him?

He got up and walked to the door. 'I'd better get an early night. Will you make sure I'm up by eight? I've got to be at school at nine.'

His father waved. 'I'll wake you, don't worry. Sleep well.'

His mother hadn't said anything, and he felt a rush inside him to put things right – it hurt so much when she showed disapproval. 'Good night, Mum. Would you like me to make you a drink before I go up?'

'No thanks,' she said, not looking up. 'Good night.'

His body felt heavy and tired after all the exertion of the day, but as he lay in bed, his mind raced. He tried various positions, forcing himself away from thinking of anything bad, but the effort made him more awake than ever. He turned over on to his back and stared upwards into the dark.

He thought about the game the next day and imagined himself playing a brilliant game, then dismissed the picture as being too corny and unlikely. But it kept coming back to him – scoring the winning goal or laying on the perfect pass for someone else to score. That was better, being a hero without actually being the centre of attraction. Goodness, he was so vain, in the sneakiest possible way. But then surely everybody dreamed things like that. Or was he the only one who was so self-centred and concerned with himself? It was impossible to tell, and yet from the outside nobody else seemed to have those kind of thoughts.

Out of nowhere the plan of writing the letter to the police came rushing back to him. He'd have a go at it tomorrow afternoon. What had he decided to put in it? He couldn't remember, so he worked it out again and pictured what it would look like. He'd have to wear gloves and use a clean sheet of paper to paste the letters on to. Perhaps if he was lucky, he could find whole words to cut out. If he had to use individual letters, it would take ages. Either way, he would have to be dead careful. Where would he post it from? He'd just go to the station and look at the time-table and see which was the furthest place he could go to and back in an afternoon – Sunday afternoon would be best. Everybody would be busy doing things then or simply resting after lunch. He could say that he was going out to see some people and perhaps have a kick around – he could be gone for three to four hours without being noticed. That didn't give him long, but it might work.

Perhaps they'd go and visit his grandmother in hospital – that would get them out of the way. He wondered whether she would be all right. What was the matter with her? Cancer? He tried to imagine what it would be like if she died. She was a really great person. He'd always got on with her and found it easy to talk to her, much easier than his parents, actually. She wouldn't die – it was just probably something little, and they wouldn't even have to operate. Perhaps Mrs Chalmers had had cancer and didn't know it and only had a few weeks left anyway. Perhaps it was meant to happen – perhaps he'd saved her suffering a painful death. His desire to wriggle out of the responsibility of his actions by imagining ridiculous things – that killing her had been doing her a favour – appalled him. He really was crazy. Supposing he said a prayer for his grandmother? She might get better. But he never prayed except when he wanted things and he knew that wasn't what you were supposed to do. Still, he would try it. He slipped out of bed and knelt on the floor. Nothing happened, no words came. He just saw himself kneeling on the floor, trying to be holy.

He got back into bed. Still his mind buzzed with activity, but no actual thoughts came to him, and he felt himself grow away from his body, and it was as if his brain was all there was to him – shrunken up and little at the top of his head – and nothing else was him, except that he could taste something sweet in his mouth . . .

He woke up three times in the night but found it easy to slip back into sleep. When his father pushed his shoulder and said, 'There's a cup of tea for you – it's about ten to eight,' he knew that he had been very deeply asleep. He managed to mumble

'O.K. Thanks', but he really wanted to turn over and slide back into the darkness. At last he forced his eyes open a little and leant over and took a sip of tea. He loved Saturdays – his dad always brought him a cup of tea, and it was a good start to the day. Saturday! The memory came back to him in a burst that jolted him awake. The game was this morning, and his heart began to beat fast in anticipation.

Fourteen

He opened the door and called out ' 'Bye!' His mother didn't answer, perhaps she hadn't heard him, but his father shouted, 'Good luck! Play well!'

'If I play. 'Bye.' He closed the door and started walking fast along the road. It had taken him ages to get going this morning, probably because he'd slept so soundly, and even though he'd gulped down his breakfast, there was only a quarter of an hour to get to school before the group left. It was another bright day, although there was still a trace of haze in the sky which the sun hadn't yet burned off. It would be perfect for football – fine yet crisp, and not a breath of wind. He mentally checked that he had put all the kit into his shoulder-bag and had a momentary jerk of panic as he wondered if he had forgotten his boots, but a quick squeeze of the canvas told him that he hadn't.

When he reached the school road, he trotted along it just to make sure, and he felt a sense of relief when he turned into the playground and saw the waiting vehicle. Mr Raines was ticking off people's names as they got on to it. Ray looked along the aisle and saw that Dave wasn't there yet, so he waved and smiled at the others and sat down in the front next to a window and looked across the playground to the school gates. No one. He glanced at his watch, nearly nine. He wondered if Dave would make it.

Someone called out, 'Hey, you'll be playing as captain if Dave doesn't turn up, Ray!'

He turned round and knelt on the seat. 'Has anyone seen him?'

'No!'

'Oh, he'll make it – he always cuts it fine,' said Ian Turner.

'You're a fine one to talk,' called Mr Raines from the entrance step. Then he said to the driver, 'Give it a couple of minutes more.'

'O.K.,' mumbled the driver, 'but it'll take a good half hour.'

Ray looked out of the window again and wouldn't allow himself to think what he knew was lurking at the back of his mind.

'Why don't we drive along the road and pick him up on the way?' suggested Chris Gilligan.

'No, it's all right – here he is,' Ray shouted with relief. Dave had just turned the corner and was running across towards them.

'Sorry I'm late,' he panted as he climbed up, and was greeted by jeers and catcalls. He smiled at the noise and bowed. 'Come on,' he said, 'I'm doing you a favour. It's our lucky charm – if I'm one minute late, we'll win the match. It's happened every time so far.'

'Yes, we'd noticed.' Mr Raines' voice tried to sound hard, but he could never manage to talk to Dave without a smile. 'Right, let's go.'

The mini-bus started forward, and Dave crashed down next to Ray. 'Hi!'

'Hi yourself. That was pretty close – I thought you weren't going to make it.'

'What a hope – I'd have to be dead before I missed a game. How are you feeling?'

'Fine.'

'Nervous?'

'No. I just hope I get a chance to play, that's all.'

Dave crammed his bag under his seat and looked back at the others. 'Well, what's it going to be – four-nil?'

'To them?' Chris asked.

'No way, mates. We've got to win this one – they're the only other unbeaten team in the league.'

'That's what he meant,' called Ian.

Dave groaned. 'Blimey, nothing like confidence.' He turned round and sat down again. The noise of the talking died down, and Ray felt the tension rise. It was going to be an important game, and everybody probably felt as nervous as he did.

The driver was right – there were a great number of cars going into the city, probably for Saturday-morning shopping – and the journey was slow. Ray kept looking down at his watch to see if they would make it in time. The Harrison High School was right on the opposite side of the city and they were making slow progress even though they were on the ring road.

Dave must have noticed his edginess, because he nudged him and said in a low tone, 'Thought you said you weren't nervous.'

'I'm not really. I was just checking to see if we'd get there on time.'

'Yes, just checking about eight times in the last five minutes. Relax.'

'Aren't you nervous?'

'No, we'll get there.'

'I mean about the game.'

'Bit.'

'That's where the Harrison lot'll be this afternoon,' shouted Fitzgerald the goalkeeper. Ray followed everybody's eyes and saw the large cemetery they were passing. A few people laughed and then they all looked away, but Ray stared out at the huge area of graves and noticed a funeral car driving slowly down the centre road towards the chapel in the middle. Perhaps it was her. How long was it before they buried people? Two or three days probably. It could be her. Except they might have done an autopsy on the body to discover the exact cause of death – in which case she might be buried later than usual. He sat brooding while he dragged pictures through his mind of coroners, courts, and mortuaries.

'Nearly there,' he heard Mr Raines say, and he snapped

back to the present and joined the others looking out for a glimpse of the school.

'There are the grounds.' Dave nodded towards the green spaces on their right. 'Look good.'

The coach turned into the school's drive and pulled up in front of the main building. It was newer than their school and had a huge gym on the edge of the pitches. There was a burst of nervous chatter and laughter as they piled from the coach and followed Mr Raines, who had met a teacher from the school and was walking towards the gym talking to him. When they reached the building the other teacher pointed to a door and said, 'Your changing-room is on the right just inside. You've got ten minutes so be as quick as you can.'

Everybody was silent as they changed into their kit and sat tying the laces on their boots. Finally Dave said, 'Right, you lot, let's go.' It was good to be out in the fresh air, and Ray felt better as he trotted with the others towards the pitch. The Harrison team was already there, kicking a couple of balls around, and there were about forty or fifty supporters standing along the touch-line. The turf was springy as Ray sprinted across the field, warming up. He saw the referee walking to the centre, calling the two captains together, and he trotted towards Mr Raines who was standing on the touch-line while the teams moved towards their positions.

'Where's your track suit, Ray?'

'I haven't got one, sir.'

'You'll get cold standing around like that – you should have borrowed one. Here, slip my coat on – I won't be wearing it.' He held out a tweed overcoat.

'No, it's all right, I'll be . . .'

'Do as I say. I don't want you stiff or shivering if I need you. Put it on.'

'I'll feel a twit with a coat on.'

'I don't care what you feel as long as you're not cold. Put it on.'

Ray put the coat on reluctantly and looked down at his bare legs which looked ridiculous below the coat. Then the whistle blew, and he forgot about what he looked like and concentrated on the game. He made up his mind to study all the Harrison players carefully, because he wanted to know what he was up against if he was put on to play.

The teams were very evenly matched, and play flowed regularly up and down the pitch with neither side winning domination. Skilful football was being played by both teams, and Ray forgot to watch for their opponents' strengths and weaknesses as the excitement of the struggle absorbed him. He and Mr Raines were the only non-playing representatives from their school, so they both shouted encouragement to the team in the face of the quite considerable support yelled by the other spectators for the Harrison team.

After half an hour, there was still no score, though both sides had had a couple of chances to take the lead. Then the Harrison team began to gain the advantage. Their right winger, a slight but fast boy, was beginning to make dangerous runs down the far touch-line and Doug Gibbons, who tried to mark him, was being beaten nearly every time.

Ray heard Mr Raines say, 'He's good', as the winger slipped Doug again and then pulled back a beautiful cross to the far post which Fitzgerald only just managed to snatch out of the air as a Harrison forward jumped for it.

Mr Raines whistled and said, 'They're getting close.' Then he shouted, 'Come on, Vermont Road – push up!'

The red shirts of the Vermont Road team surged up field as Fitzgerald kicked deep into the Harrison half, but a blue-shirted defender reached the ball first and passed it accurately out to the right wing again – they too had obviously spotted where their superiority was. The winger started his run down the line, and Doug Gibbons moved towards him to try and cut him out. The winger kept coming and Doug backed off, trying to force him to commit himself and then make the tackle. But with a little flick to the right, the winger was past him and was accelerating in towards the goal. He swerved past another red shirt, and was in the penalty area. His left-foot shot was perfect and although Fitzgerald dived and got a hand to it, the ball skidded into the net.

Ray groaned and glanced at Mr Raines, who stood impassively gazing towards the centre spot as the players re-grouped for the kick-off. The last few minutes of the first half were all Vermont Road's, with Dave pushing his team forward with good passes from mid-field, but the Harrison defence was sound and managed to smother the attacks without there being even one shot at goal. The whistle blew for half-time, and Ray and Mr Raines walked on to the pitch towards the team.

'O.K. Sit down and rest,' said their coach, and the team sat or squatted to listen to what he had to say. Ray felt out of it for the first time as he realized that the advice Mr Raines was giving was for the team, not for the 12th man who was watching it from the side-lines. He turned and went over to get the plate of quartered oranges that a boy was bringing over. When he got back to the group the players took the oranges and sucked greedily on them. 'Flipping tea-boy,' he thought as he held out the plate for the peel.

'Right,' said Mr Raines, 'forwards, remember to run into space. Don't wait for the ball and then try and get past a defender. They're not playing the offside trap so go past them *for* the ball, not *with* it. That applies especially to you, Peter.' He turned towards Doug Gibbons. 'Their only real threat is that winger, Doug – and he's your responsibility. Don't back off – go in and worry him. O.K.?' Doug nodded, and Mr Raines and Ray walked back to the touch-line as the referee blew the whistle to get the teams ready for the second half.

Ray put down the plate and shivered – it was cold even with that stupid coat.

'Cold, Ray?'

'A bit.'

'Well, jog up and down the line to get warm – we may need you.'

He didn't need to be told twice. As he trotted backwards and forwards watching the play, he filled with hope. It was slower this half, and both sides seemed to be playing safe, as though afraid to make mistakes. Then twice in succession a pass from mid-field to behind the Harrison defenders gave the Vermont Road forwards a chance as they ran on to the ball: once the shot was very wide, and the second was palmed over by the goalkeeper for a corner.

'Raines really knows his football,' Ray thought, watching his team fight for another opening. The Harrison team was tiring, and after about twenty-five minutes a beautiful pass from Dave split their defence, and Peter Loughton ran on to the ball and swept it wide of the keeper and into the far corner of the net. The half-time advice had paid off, and the teams were even again at 1–1.

The game restarted. It was obvious that the Harrison team still hadn't spotted the tactics, because twice more the Vermont Road forwards ran on to through-balls and came near to scoring. Then with about fifteen minutes left to play, the ball ran loose, and a blue shirt flicked it out to the winger. He burst into a run, easily evading Doug's despairing tackle, and sent a low hard cross right across the goal. A Harrison forward jabbed at it and missed. The ball ran off for a goal kick, but it had been a very close thing.

Ray felt Mr Raines tap him on the shoulder. 'Let me have my coat back. I'm sending you on and calling Gibbons off. Now watch that number seven – he's fast. Go into him, don't let him get in another cross like that.' Ray nodded and began jumping up and down to loosen up as Mr Raines held up his hand to attract the referee's attention. The ball went out of play and the game was stopped to allow the substitution to take place. Mr Raines pointed to Doug who was already walking towards them as though he realized that it was bound to be him. Mr Raines grabbed Ray's shoulder as he prepared to run on. 'Firm,' he said and then looked straight into Ray's eyes, 'but fair, I don't want anything dirty.' Then he tapped him on the back, and Ray ran across the pitch, and play restarted. Dave winked at him as he passed. He turned towards the action and became aware of the dryness of his mouth – if only he had some chewing-gum.

He walked up towards the centre-line as his forwards took the play up to the Harrison goal. He watched the ball slide from one red-shirted player to another until a shot was blocked by a defender and scuttled off for a corner. He glanced over to the touch-line and saw Mr Raines signalling him to move up for the kick. He sprinted up and joined the seven other red shirts waiting for the corner to be taken. Paul Farmer was taking it, and Ray began to trot into the penalty area as the ball flew up towards the centre. But it was too long – it sailed over everyone's head and rolled off harmlessly for a goal kick. He raced back into his own half and watched the goalkeeper run up and boot the ball long and high. Ray knew where it was aimed, and sure enough, he saw the right winger trap it elegantly and begin to move towards him.

He was coming fast – faster here than it had looked when he had been watching from the side. Ray began to trot backwards as the winger advanced. Then he suddenly remembered his instructions and stopped and moved in towards his man. The winger paused as though unsure of what to do. Ray lunged out with his right foot, and as he did so, the ball was pushed inside him, and the winger burst past him after it. He scrambled to his feet and gave chase, but he was five yards behind him. He saw that left foot rise and watched hopelessly as the ball shot towards goal. But it was just wide, clipped the post, and went rocketing out of play. Ray clenched his fist and determined not to let it happen again.

Fitzgerald took the kick, and the ball sailed over into the Harrison half. It was won by a blue shirt, and the attack began to build up again. The ball was swept up to the other wing this time, and all the players moved over in that direction –

but Ray stayed where he was, guarding that flank against the real danger. The ball was in amongst a mass of players, but suddenly it came out, and a Harrison player kicked it far out towards Ray's side. It was a superb move, because all the players were clustered together on the other side of the field and this sudden switch left only Ray and that winger with a chance for the ball – and if the winger got past him this time, there was a clear run at goal.

The ball bounced, and Ray and the winger ran towards it. As he neared it, Ray knew that the other player was just going to get to it first – it was going to be close but the winger had the speed and Ray knew with certainty that he would miss it. He flung himself full stretch and lifted his foot slightly – if he couldn't get the ball, then at least he could get the player – and by sheer luck his foot caught the ball first. It spun off towards touch, but his impetus carried him through, and he caught the winger's leg half-way up his shin. The other player went down heavily on his side.

As Ray got to his feet, he heard the Harrison spectators booing. The referee ran over and looked down at the boy on the ground who was clutching his leg and rolling in pain.

Ray walked over and tried to apologize to the boy, but the referee pushed him away and bent down to examine the leg. Ray could see the red marks that his studs had left on the shin, and he felt the bitterness build up in him. He had won the ball and probably saved the game, but he had done it in the wrong way. He had thrown away his chance with the team – Mr Raines was always strict about dirty play and had even given him that extra warning just before he had come on. The few boos that still sounded across the field turned to cheers as the winger hobbled to his feet and limped off the field. The referee walked towards Ray with his finger raised. 'Any more tackles like that and you're off,' he said. Then he pointed to the spot where the free kick was to be taken.

Ray walked back towards the goal, feeling wretched. A Harrison player took the kick, and the ball came high towards him.

Automatically he rose and headed it perfectly, and the ball flew into touch. He heard Fitzgerald yell, 'Well done', but the excitement and pleasure had drained out of him. From the throw-in, a Vermont Road player won the ball, and the red shirts moved upfield again, leaving Ray behind. The last few minutes' play were all in the Harrison half, and Ray had nothing more to do. Then the whistle blew, and it was all over. He ran straight towards the winger who was limping across the pitch. 'I'm sorry,' he said. 'Are you O.K.?'

'Yeah, I'll be all right.'

'I'm really sorry – I didn't mean it.'

'Not much,' sneered the winger.

As Ray left the field, one or two of the younger boys from the school booed him and he lowered his head in shame. Then he felt Mr Raines' hand on his shoulder. 'Don't worry. It was a perfectly fair tackle. It was a fifty-fifty ball, and you won it.' Ray looked up. Mr Raines was smiling. 'You did well,' he added. 'Forget it.'

Ray's despair lifted – and he looked directly at his P.E. teacher. 'But the ref blamed me – he told me that he'd send me off.'

'Refs make mistakes. It was perfectly fair. You got the ball, didn't you?'

'Yes.'

'Well, there you are then.' Mr Raines smiled again and patted him on the back. 'You did well.'

Ray smiled and then ran off towards the rest of the team. As he reached them, Dave called out, 'Well done, mate – fantastic tackle!' The others nodded and began talking about how well he'd done.

The pain lifted, and Ray realized that what he had dreamed about had happened – he'd saved the game. The unfairness of his tackle threw a shadow over it, but it seemed as if only he knew about that, and if he kept quiet about it, then it was happiness. Of a sort.

Fifteen

He joined in all the after-game laughter and shouting in the showers and on the trip back. The team were happy with the result, feeling that it was an achievement to have held their main opponents in the league to a draw. Mr Raines was obviously pleased and said it had been a good match – and the team responded to his praise with a lot of joking and boasting about the game. Ray was made to feel a part of the team and gratefully agreed to go to the party that was being arranged for that evening at Chris Gilligan's house, since Chris's parents were going out and he told everybody that he'd ring round some people in the afternoon to invite them to 'the orgy!'

The happy mood stayed with Ray as he walked from the school with Dave discussing the game yet again and getting another lift of pleasure when Dave praised the way he had played for the short time he'd been on. As they parted at the corner of Dave's road, Ray gave him some money to buy a big bottle of cheap wine between them for the party.

Ray's good mood was not matched by the atmosphere of gloom that hung about the house when he got home. He went into the kitchen, full of his news and ready to tell them about his success, and he was met by a feeling of tension. His mother was sitting tight-lipped and pale at the table, and Derek was leaning against the door with an angry, sulky look on his face. His father stood at the stove frying some sausages. Nobody spoke or even glanced at Ray as he stood in the doorway. His stomach sank, and his heart pounded as he sensed the mood of the room – for one terrible moment he thought that they had found out about him, that the police had been, and everybody knew the truth. He was seized with a sudden desire to run and had even begun to turn away to get out when his father looked round and said, 'Hello. How did you get on?' His voice was rather mechanical and didn't seem very enthusiastic, but Ray breathed with relief – he'd never ask something like that if they had found out about the accident.

'Oh it was great. It was a draw, one-all. I played for about twenty minutes.'

'Good.' Again there was no excitement in the voice. Ray was bursting to talk about the game, had looked forward to telling them about the winger and the tackle, but something was up. His grandmother? Perhaps she was worse. He was just going to ask about her, when he remembered that Derek was not supposed to know about it. He glanced at his brother, who was still standing moodily against the door. Why was he in such a bad temper if it was still being kept a secret from him?

'What's the matter?' he asked, but nobody replied. 'Has something happened?' he added to try and break through the silence.

His father started serving the sausages. 'No. It's nothing. Just a bit of a tiff, that's all. Come and sit down and have your lunch. And you, Derek.'

Ray sat at the table next to his mother, who was staring straight ahead of her. He wondered if she was still upset about what he'd said the night before. His father put the plates of sausages, potatoes and peas on the table, ran some water over the pans in the sink, and then sat down. 'Come on, Derek,' he urged, 'come and eat your lunch.'

Derek shook his head and looked at the floor.

'Come on. Come and sit down next to me, and eat your sausages,' his father repeated, but still the young boy stayed against the door and Ray realized that whatever was wrong had something to do with his brother.

'Leave him alone.' It was his mother, her voice cold and snapping. 'If he doesn't want to eat, then he can starve.' She picked up her knife and fork and slashed at the food in anger.

'I hate you!' shouted Derek and burst into tears. He banged the door with the side of his fist and ran out of the room. Ray heard the clumps as his brother stamped up the stairs, and he was suddenly embarrassed as he remembered his own behaviour a couple of days before. At the same time he felt sympathy for Derek – their mother could be really hurtful when she was in a mood. However, all the trouble had nothing to do with him, and the relief of that relaxed him so that he began to eat hungrily. It was his favourite lunch, and this was the first time that he'd really felt hungry for the last couple of days.

After a couple of minutes, his father picked up Derek's plate and put it in the oven to keep warm. It was still silent and tense round the table, so Ray began talking about the game. He hated it when there was trouble in the family so he talked quickly describing the whole game, trying to cover up the silence. When it came to the part about the tackle, he even used the salt and pepper pots to show the position of the players and he put as much enthusiasm into his voice as he could – not that that was difficult because as he retold it he felt a glow of pride. He briefly mentioned that the winger had been hurt, but he quickly added, 'Still, it couldn't be helped. You know, it was one of those fifty-fifty balls, and it was just an accident that someone got hurt. He was O.K. anyway, really, just a few grazes. And everyone said afterwards that they thought it had been a fair tackle and they didn't blame me. And it probably saved a goal too.'

His father nodded and tried to seem interested, but Ray could see that he was still upset by whatever had happened. His mother said nothing and ate only part of her lunch. Ray reached the end of his story and could think of nothing else to say, so he finished his meal in silence.

At last his mother pushed her plate away and stood up. 'We'll have to go in a minute. I'll get ready.' She walked out of the kitchen and closed the door.

'What's happened?' whispered Ray as soon as his mother had left the room.

His father sighed deeply and began to collect the plates together. 'Oh, it's been a hell of a morning. Your grandmother was much worse when we took her to hospital, and I think she's very ill. She looks terribly thin, and I think that she'll probably have to have an operation. She's still quite cheerful, of course, because she's not the sort to let it get her down. But it was really grim, and it upset your mother a lot.' He stood up and carried the things to the sink. Ray began to clear the table. 'Then when we got home, we found out that Derek had been a bit of a nuisance and had had a fight with Mrs Walker's son, and your mother just lost her temper with him.'

'I'll do the washing-up,' said Ray. 'Where are you going now?'

'Well, we've got to go back to the hospital this afternoon.' He paused. 'Are you going to be in, Ray?'

'Yes, I expect so.'

'Do you think you could stay in and look after Derek? We can't take him with us, and we can't ask Mrs Walker to have him, of course.'

Ray was anxious to reassure his father. 'Sure, I'm not doing anything. He'll be O.K. with me. Look, if you've got to go, I'll finish this. You go and get ready.'

His father looked at him and began to dry his hands on the towel. 'Thanks a lot, Ray. I think things are going to be a bit tough while your grandmother is ill. Your mother will be upset, and we'll all have to try and help as much as possible. It's good to know that you'll help.'

Ray felt pleased at his words, but at the same time the thought of the agony that hung over all their heads filled him with horror. What with everything else, they'd never be able to cope with things if they knew the truth about what he had done. His father spoke to him as if he could help them through their troubles but he didn't know that he was more likely to destroy them all.

'Right. We'll be off now. I won't go and see Derek – it's best to leave him to cool off for a while. Perhaps you can persuade him to eat his lunch after we've gone.'

'O.K., Dad. See you later. I hope everything's all right.'

He carried on washing-up while his father left the room and when he had dried everything and was putting away the saucepans he heard the front door slam as they left for the hospital. It was a stroke of luck, really. Now no one was likely to disturb him while he prepared the letter – and he'd probably need a lot of stuff in order to get it done.

He went into the front room and got a writing-pad and an envelope out of the sideboard drawer, then pulled some newspapers off the pile in the cupboard under the stairs. He needed some glue, too, and he found some in the outside shed and the scissors in his mother's work-basket. He picked up all the stuff and carried it upstairs and dropped it on to his bed. Then he opened Derek's door. The young boy was lying on the floor reading a comic.

'Are you going to eat your dinner? It's in the oven, nice and warm.'

Derek looked up, and his face was still puffy and tear-stained. 'No!'

'Oh, come on, Derek. Mum and Dad have gone out. You may as well eat it. You'll be hungry if you don't.

'No!'

'Suit yourself then.' He closed the door, went back to his own room and sat down on the bed. What was he going to put in the letter? As he tried to think of things he could say, he was once more filled with doubts about the whole idea. All the phrases and sentences he thought of seemed so ridiculous. The letter would just look what it was – an attempt by someone to throw the police off the track. Then he remembered the way his father had looked at him earlier and he knew he had to try anything he could think of to keep from bringing disaster on his family. With this thought uppermost in his mind, he quickly chose a couple of short sentences and set about looking for the words that he needed.

Turning the pages of the first newspaper, he soon found some of the more common words that he could use and began to cut them out and lay them in order. It was much easier than he had imagined. In about twenty-five minutes he had only three gaps left in the line of words. He knew where he could fill one of the gaps. He went downstairs and got the local paper which had the story of the accident in it and cut out the words 'Mrs Chalmers' from the article. It was a risk – but one that had to be taken – he just hoped that nobody would miss the page, which he had made up his mind he would burn in the boiler along with the other pages that he had cut words out of.

That left just two words to find and he began scanning the newspapers again. After about fifteen minutes he found them both in the same story. It was an article that he remembered reading nearly two weeks earlier – the story of a young mother who had beaten her baby to death because it had cried all night, and who had then killed herself. At the time, he had been filled with disgust at her cruelty and stupidity, but now he read the story with new eyes. A shudder of terror shook him. Then he cut out the two words he needed – 'disgrace' and 'suicide'.

He bundled the cut pages together and crushed them into a ball. Down in the kitchen, he opened the boiler door and threw them in and watched as they started to burn. He put the rest of the papers back under the stairs and then got the pink kitchen-gloves from the drawer next to the sink. Back in his room he put on the gloves and wiped both sides of the pieces he had cut from the papers just in case he had left any prints on them. He opened the writing-pad and tore out the second-to-last page, guessing that it was the least likely to have any marks on it. He began sticking the words on to the sheet, and when they were all on, he waved it around to dry the glue. He laid it down on the bed. It looked really messy, but that didn't matter, nor did the fact that all the words were of different sizes. It read:

I killed Mrs Chalmers. It was an accident. I have decided to commit suicide. I cannot live any longer, the disgrace will kill my wife.

He folded it up and slipped it into the envelope. The bit about the wife was brilliant – it would change the whole age of the person they were looking for. They were bound to have thought it was a young person who had stolen the bike, but this would lead them off in another direction entirely. He was just going to lick the envelope when he thought that it was just possible that they could even get clues from spit; so he went into the bathroom, wet his glove under the tap, and ran the finger along the sticky strip.

Now there was the problem of the address – he could hardly stick bits of newspaper on the outside, besides it would be impossible to find the words. He got a blue ball-point pen and began to print the words, holding the pen in his left hand in order to disguise the writing even more. He didn't know the full address, so he just put 'The City Police Station' and then the city and the county – it was bound to be delivered to the right place and anyway it would look more like someone from outside the area who didn't know the right address. He looked the envelope over – the words were very shaky and uneven, but it would have to do. It occurred to him that he could have printed the letter too, but he decided that the cut-out words were even safer because the more he had written the more the handwriting experts would have to go on.

He gathered together all the things he had used and took them downstairs and put them back in their places, then went back to his room. After all the concentration, he felt very tired, and he put the letter inside his football magazine and left it on the table next to his bed. He opened the door in order to make sure that he knew what Derek was doing – he didn't want any trouble while he was supposed to be in charge of him. Then he lay down on the bed and closed his eyes.

He thought about the party in the evening. Would there be many people there? Probably. Chris was good at organizing things and people never had much to do at the week-ends and would welcome the change of a party. It was strange how they all always talked about having parties, but how rarely they actually did. It was always such a problem to know where to hold parties – it was no good if there were parents about.

When he woke up, the light was already growing dim in his room and he realized that it was late in the afternoon. He was cold and he folded half the eiderdown over the top of himself. His eyes were heavy, and he found it difficult to open them – he must have slept very deeply. That game had taken quite a lot out of him and he hadn't had much sleep for the last three nights. He pulled his arm from under the covers and looked at his watch – just gone 5.30. He had been asleep for nearly two and a half hours. He wondered whether his parents were back yet and he listened to see if he could hear anything. There were no sounds from the kitchen, but he could hear music from the television. Derek had come out of his room, obviously, and had gone down to watch it. He'd better get up and check that he was not doing anything wrong.

Ray stretched, rolled off the bed, and stumbled to the door. Then as he was leaving the room, he glanced back and saw that the magazine had gone.

He turned back and flicked on the light. It wasn't on the table where he had left it, and he ducked down to see if it had fallen off under the bed. The magazine wasn't there – nor was the letter.

Panic began to rise in him. He ran down the stairs and burst into the front room. Derek was lying on the floor as usual, watching the TV, and his dinner plate was next to him empty – but there was no sign of the magazine.

Ray's voice was urgent and uncontrolled, almost breaking, as he half-shouted, 'Where is it? Have you taken my magazine?'

Derek looked up, surprised. 'What?'

'My magazine. My football magazine – have you taken it?'

'I only borrowed it.'

'Well, where on earth is it?'

'It's in my room. I finished my comic and I didn't have anything to read. And you were asleep so I . . .'

'Don't you ever dare to take things from my room, or I'll belt you.' Ray crashed the door to and ran upstairs and into Derek's room. The magazine lay on the floor, open at the first page. He picked it up and flicked wildly through it. The letter was still there, right in the middle where he'd put it. He fumbled it over and saw that it hadn't been opened. That dreadful kid.

He took the letter back to his room and looked around for somewhere to hide it. Then suddenly he realized that he was holding it in his bare hands – it would have his finger-prints all over it, and perhaps Derek's too. He got out his handkerchief and wiped both sides, holding it between the cloth. Wiping it smudged the ink a bit, but at least it would destroy any prints that could be traced.

He opened a book and put it inside, then laid them both away under his clothes in the wardrobe drawer. It would be safe there until tomorrow. But had Derek seen the letter? The magazine was only open at the first page – he may not have read the whole thing. How on earth could he find out without making it obvious? Especially now. The kid had been in a bad mood before, but now that Ray had shouted at him he would be even more uncooperative.

He went back to the front room, and he could tell immediately that Derek was in a bad temper, by the way he was lying on the floor. Ray sat down on the sofa and watched the television for about five mintes before he forced himself to say, 'Derek.' His brother remained silent and unmoving. 'Derek, I'm sorry I lost my temper with you.' Still the young boy didn't look round. 'It was just that there was something important in the magazine.' He thought desperately of what to say. 'Something somebody lent me – a letter they had written.' It was clumsy, but he felt that he had to refer directly to it in order to get anywhere. 'It was a joke letter that they were go-

ing to use for the party tonight. We're going to play a game.'
He wanted to cover himself with a reasonable explanation if
Derek had seen it. 'We're going to play a game of "Murder" at
the party. And the letter was part of the game.' He paused.
Derek still hadn't moved or spoken. 'And it was important, and
I just didn't want to lose it. Anyway, I'm sorry.' He was
floundering around and the explanation was getting weaker
with every word. Then Derek mumbled something.

'What?' Ray's hopes rose.

'I didn't do anything.'

'No, I know you didn't. I said I was sorry – I just lost my
temper, that's all.'

'I only wanted something to read – and then I decided to
watch the telly.'

'Didn't you read it then?' He could barely keep the hope out
of his voice. 'I'll let you borrow it. Didn't you read it?'

'I only read a bit.'

'Well, I'll let you borrow it, and you can read it.' The time
had come for the real question, but it seemed such a big step
even though the conversation so far had been encouraging. He
paused, then got it out in a burst: 'So you didn't even see it
then? The letter?'

'No. I only was going to read the magazine. I didn't know
it was anything special.' His voice was still sulky and self-
pitying and Ray knew that he was telling the truth.

'Well, it doesn't matter anyway – you can borrow it.' He
wanted to please his brother and cancel any memory out of his
mind. 'You can have it, and, if you want any of the pictures,
you can cut them out and put them on your wall. There are
some good ones. O.K.?'

'Can I?' Derek's young face lit up with pleasure, and Ray
saw that it had been a bad day for him and that it would be
easy to please him just by being nice.

'Sure. And you can borrow any of the ones I get. You can
share them with me every week.'

'I don't want my comics any more, but Mum says I can't

have football magazines because they cost too much.'

'Well, in future you can share mine *and* have your comics.'

'Thanks.' Derek was now anxious to please in return. 'City won today. I saw it on the results. They beat Wolves 3–1.'

'Great!' Ray exaggerated his excitement to please his brother. 'I see you've eaten your dinner. Are you ready for some tea? I'm starving. I'll make some for both of us, O.K.?'

The boy nodded, and Ray got up and went out into the kitchen. He put the kettle on and began cutting some bread. He felt close to Derek, and it pleased him to make him happy – it was so obvious that he was really upset about what had happened all day. Poor kid, first there was the trouble with Mum, and then all the fuss over a magazine. They really ought to tell him about Grandma – he was bright, he could understand. It would be so much easier to know rather than to be left in the dark.

He piled the plates and the bread and butter on to a tray and added cheese and jam and peanut butter. Then he made the tea and put the pot on the tray. It would be good to sit together in front of the TV and eat their teas – and it would please Derek not to miss any programmes. What a TV addict he was! Thinking of the good feeling that had suddenly developed between them, Ray smiled – and the moment was only slightly marred by the realization that it had simply suited his needs to keep the boy happy.

He carried the tea to the front room, and they sat together and ate and drank and talked about football and discussed the programmes they watched. An hour and a half passed quickly, and Ray felt that he was really getting to know his brother for the first time.

When their parents came in just before seven both boys were surprised at how quickly the time had gone. Derek acted as though he had forgotten that he had been in disgrace earlier. Ray made a big thing of telling his parents how well Derek had behaved and what a good time they had had together. The mood of contentment and peace seemed to affect their parents too, and they chatted and smiled and asked questions in a completely different way from the tension of lunchtime. Their father had bought the local paper and Ray let Derek look at it first while he loaded the tea things on to the tray and followed his parents out into the kitchen.

'Sorry we've been so long,' whispered his mother as she closed the door, 'but we had to go back to Grandma's after the hospital and tidy up a few things.'

'That's O.K. We've had a good time.'

'Well, Derek seems much better, I must say. Thanks a lot, Ray.' His father smiled and added, 'We've got everything settled now. Was he any bother? I see he's eaten his dinner.'

'No, he was fine. I think he was probably just a bit confused about what was going on.' Then he saw that this might be a dangerous line to follow, knowing his mother, so he quickly changed the subject. 'Do you think it'll be O.K. for me to go to a party tonight at Chris's place? It's a sort of celebration after the game.'

He saw that his mother was going to start asking questions about it, but his father cut in straight away and said, 'Of course you can. I wouldn't mind a party myself to cheer us up. Yes, of course you can go – especially after looking after Derek so well for us. Can't he, love?'

Ray's mother gave him a look and nodded. 'I don't mind, I'm sure. How many people are going?'

'Oh, not many – it's just a sort of get-together, that's all.'

'Who's going?'

'Just the team.'

She was about to ask some more questions, but again his father interrupted. 'Well, you'd better go and get ready – and we'll get ourselves some tea.' He looked directly at Ray and nodded to the door. 'Go on, hurry up or you'll never get there on time.' Ray saw what his father was doing and nodded.

'Yeah, I'll have to hurry.'

He went upstairs and washed. His father could be pretty sharp about things sometimes.

He put on his green cords and a tee-shirt, then chose a brown sweater to wear. He went back into the bathroom and brushed his teeth, then looked closely at his face in the mirror. Should he shave off the hairs round his chin yet or not? He turned sideways and tried to see what he looked like in profile, then examined himself full-face again. No, he'd leave it for a while – he'd look too much of a kid if he didn't have that hair, even though it wasn't much yet. He took his father's after-shave lotion and splashed some on his face and sweater. He might not shave yet, but at least he could smell as if he did. He combed his hair a couple of times, trying to decide which style suited him best, and then ended up by just mussing it up with his fingers – it looked better if it was a bit wild and curly. It ought to be a bit longer, too. He brushed the flecks from his shoulder, had a last look at himself in the mirror, then went back to his room. He picked up his denim jacket and put some money in the top pocket. He had a quick look in his drawer just to check that the book was well-hidden, then switched off the light, closed his door and went downstairs.

His parents were in the kitchen drinking tea. 'Let's have a look at you. Mm, not bad,' said his mother. 'Are you off now?'

'Yes – I'd better go, it's nearly eight.'

'Well, what time will you be home?'

'I don't know. Not very late. But don't wait up – I've got my key.'

'Yes, well, don't be too late,' his mother said. 'I think you ought to be back by eleven-thirty.'

'O.K. I'll see you in the morning. Don't bother to wake me – I'll probably sleep late.'

'Have a good time. Your mother and I are going to the hospital again tomorrow morning so we might not see you till later. 'Bye.'

Ray put his jacket on and closed the front door. This evening he was going to forget everything and just enjoy himself.

Sixteen

By nine-thirty the wine was going to his head. Dave had bought a huge bottle of very raw Italian red wine, which nobody else drank after they'd tasted it, so Dave and Ray kept gulping it down by the glassful. It had the effect of drying their mouths, and for the last couple of glasses they had added lemonade to it. Both of them stood in the kitchen near the drinks table, with sweat beginning to break out on their foreheads. It was hot and noisy there, but not nearly as suffocating and ear-blasting as the front room.

There were about forty-five people at the party, many of whom Ray had never met before: and when he had arrived, he had quickly waved to those he knew and then had sought out Dave. Since then they had been out in the kitchen, drinking and feeling rather awkward. Because they were near the drinks table, people kept brushing past them and asking them questions like, 'What's in the punch?' or 'Is there any cider?' Only occasionally when other members of the team had come out to the kitchen, had there been a burst of conversation and shouting and laughter.

Dave and Ray seemed to be the only two who didn't know most of the people, and Ray was grateful that he had someone to talk to. When people came into the kitchen he tried to act as though he were deep in the sort of conversation that couldn't possibly be held in the chaos of the main room. Indeed for a time he and Dave had been talking, freely and happily, mostly about football and the morning's game in particular, but for the last half-hour, as the wine had fuddled their brains, the gaps in their conversation had grown longer. Then Dave said he had to go to the lavatory, and Ray was alone in the kitchen. For about ten minutes he had served drinks to anyone who came in, so that he didn't feel so obviously out of things, but then he finally picked up his drink and decided to brave the large group of people in the other room.

The air was thick with smoke and the floor packed with people either moving in time to the roaring music or standing near the walls holding shouted conversations. In the far corners some couples were sitting in chairs holding each other tight or kissing. Most of the people were two or three years older than Ray and the whole atmosphere was different from any other party he'd been to, more adult, and more sophisticated. It excited him and at the same time daunted him – he felt even more clumsy and foolish than usual at a party. Now, standing near the door, he felt that he stood out as being lonely and unwanted, and he found himself trying to smile and look totally wrapped up in the music. He thought about working his way over towards the speakers and thumbing through the records, perhaps even taking over the job of selecting and playing them. Then, as one tune ended and some bodies moved aside for a moment, he saw that the tape-recorder was being used. Chris had obviously decided not to risk his records in this crush of people and had recorded some tapes instead. It was a sensible thing to have done, but Ray was peeved. He could have looked useful and made himself a part of the scene if he'd been selecting the records.

Finally he saw Dave. He was sitting on the arm of a chair, bending forward talking to a girl. It was Rosie Newton. She was in the same year at their school, and Dave had been wanting to get to know her for months. How on earth had he plucked up the courage to talk to her now? It must have been the effect of the wine. Ray knew that he should stay away and leave the two of them alone, but he felt so desperately embarrassed on his own that he began to edge his way towards them between the swaying people. But he never made it. As he was easing past one group, Ian Turner who was talking to two girls suddenly swept an arm round him and pulled him back towards the girls.

'It's Ray, our football hero!' he shouted, sloshing some of his beer over the front of Ray's sweater. 'I'm sorry,' he said and began to wipe the beer with his hand.

'That's O.K.,' said Ray and gratefully squeezed in beside Ian, facing the two girls.

'This is Anna, and you know Jane, don't you?' Ian waved his hand unsteadily towards them, nearly spilling what was left of his beer. Jane was one of the most attractive girls at the school and Ray knew that Ian had taken her out a couple of times and wanted to make her a more permanent girl-friend but she was very popular and enjoyed having more than one boy at a time. Ray didn't like her much – she was too sure of herself and made him feel uneasy. He had never seen Anna before. She was tall, nearly his height, and she stood very straight, almost stiffly. Her hair was dark brown and hung down below her shoulders without a single curl. Her face was pale and almost thin. She looked very delicate. He liked her at once – she wasn't attractive in the usual way, but she looked gentle and quiet.

The minute he admitted his interest to himself, he felt self-conscious and timid. He had been out with two girls in the past – three dates with one and two dates with the other. He had never taken them anywhere except to the cinema, and although he had enjoyed the idea of being with a girl and had hoped to be seen, it hadn't really been much fun. He had found it very strained and awkward talking to them, and it had soon become obvious that they were not very interested in him. When he was honest with himself, he realized that he had only asked them out because he knew that it was required of him. Most of his friends had had similar short experiences and then boasted about what they had done, and only a few had regular girls, but everyone seemed to feel that they ought to try. Actually that wasn't true, there were still a large number of boys in his class who had never been out with girls and didn't seem even to care about it. But the group that he mostly mixed with certainly had, and so he had forced himself to pluck up courage to ask the two girls he had been with. And he had found that part fantastically exciting and it had filled his mind for days beforehand. Yet the dates themselves had only seemed to make him feel clumsy and false.

And that was what he felt now, but he also had the wine inside him, and his voice, at least, was free from the leaden fear that urged him to return to the kitchen and stand serving drinks. To his astonishment, he heard himself say to Anna, 'Do you want to dance?'

When she answered, 'Yes', and smiled, he saw how easy it was if only you could force yourself to do it. He put his glass of wine and lemonade under a chair and pushed himself nearer the mass of moving bodies in the centre of the floor. It was absurd – there was no room to do more than bump up and down in time to the music but that was good. Even in his semi-drunken state he would have felt terribly self-conscious if he had really to dance. She was close to him, hardly moving and keeping her head down to avoid his eyes. She was nervous too, and that made it easier. He found the corners of his mouth twitching into a smile of pleasure and his eyes watered slightly with an emotion that included happiness and relief.

The music was very loud, so there was no point in trying to talk even at this close range. When she eventually looked up at him, he just grinned, and she smiled back. It was a very long piece of music and he felt himself getting hotter even though he was barely moving. He found himself wondering what to do when the music ended. Ask for another dance? Stand at the side and talk – or rather shout – to her? The doubts began to creep into his brain again, and he cursed himself. Why was it that he could never just enjoy the moment? Why did he have to keep thinking and worrying about what was going to happen next?

The music suddenly changed into a thumping beat, and the singer began belting out a long repetitive chorus which everybody joined in, stamping their feet at the same time. He too beat harder on the ground. The noise was deafening – it must have been audible for a long way down the street outside. Suppose somebody next door complained to the police? He could have kicked himself for thinking that, because immediately his mind began to torture itself with the possibilities. Names and addresses – even questions asked – perhaps the chance word that would bring him under suspicion.

What was he trying to do to himself? His body was here at a party with a girl. He was dancing, and he should be enjoying himself. And yet here was his brain trying to ruin everything with stupid, impossible fears. It was like being two people – one of whom wanted to destroy the other with misery.

The music built to a climax, then stopped abruptly. He looked at Anna. She rolled her eyes and said, 'Phew, I'm hot.'

'Yes, so am I. Do you want a drink?'

'Please.'

'What?'

'Cider?'

'O.K., I'll get one.'

He picked up his glass and swallowed his drink, then pushed himself through the crowd towards the door. He poured himself another full glass of wine and gulped it down, then another. Then he filled his glass again. He would drive those thoughts out of himself one way or the other. He washed out another glass, which had a cigarette-end floating in some beer, and then poured some cider for her and carried the drinks back to the other room. He felt his eyes were wide and staring, and he was aware that he was swaying slightly and had to concentrate hard on not spilling the drinks as he squeezed back towards her.

As he stood talking to her, there seemed to be almost no air. He wanted to go outside and cool off, but he thought that it would seem too forward if he suggested it. He tried instead to devote his whole attention to his questions and her answers – because that was the way it was going. Either she was even more painfully shy than he was, or she was a bit stupid, because she did nothing to help him get a conversation going. It was simply a question of his asking something, then her answering as briefly as possible. She was still at school. At St John's in the centre of the city. She didn't know many people at the party. Jane had asked her to come. She knew Jane because they both had a Saturday job. At Marks and Spencers. She didn't go to many parties. She was enjoying herself.

Then a long pause. He could think of nothing else to ask, and he felt that he couldn't go on interrogating her. His mind was beginning to fog over, and he was aware that he was, for the first time ever, very drunk. But that didn't stop him drinking his glass of wine at one gulp. He forced himself to ask one more question before he gave up. And, yes, she would like another dance. They bobbed and swayed through two fast songs, and then with his eyes half-closed and his body continually lurching against other people, he put his arms right round her and held her tight for a slow dance.

Only a quarter of his brain registered what was happening, but he liked the feel of her pressed close to him – closer than he had ever held a girl before, though he was dimly aware that the heat had made them both rather damp. Chris had obviously planned his tape, because for the next twenty minutes or so, there was nothing but slow, close-dancing music. Without talking, Ray held on to Anna and swayed gently – only occasionally moving his feet. Once he caught sight of Dave, who raised his thumb and pointed with a smile at Anna's back and mouthed something that Ray took to be 'Who is it?' He just made a face and then lost sight of his friend.

He leant his head on Anna's shoulder and began a long turn in time with the music. He was terribly hot, and he could feel that his movements were drunken, but he hung on tight. Although he was drunk, he had enough awareness of what was happening to feel that he had broken through some sort of barrier. She was a girl, and he was holding her very close, and there was no embarrassment. Then somebody turned off the lights, and a faint cheer went up, and a couple of people whistled.

Anna moved her hands on his back, and he wondered if she wanted to kiss him. He moved his head off her shoulder to look at her, but she kept her face pressed against his neck, and he didn't dare force it round. Instead, with a tremble of apprehension and excitement, he pressed his lips against her hair. He could smell the shampoo she had used – or was it some sort of perfume? Whatever it was, it thrilled him as it filled his nose and he felt a rush of desire and held her tighter.

Almost immediately the music stopped, and the central light burst on glaringly. There were groans and it was switched off and replaced by the gentler glow from the standard lamp in the corner that had been on before. But still Anna stepped away from him in the absence of music and he was gripped with a feeling of faintness. He stumbled after her to the edge of the room, his head swimming alarmingly. She had found Jane again and was talking to her. He tried wildly to focus his eyes. It was no good – he'd have to get some air. He bent down and picked up his glass and almost fell as he stood up and felt the blood gush through his head.

'Just get a drink,' he mumbled and staggered to the door.

He turned left into the hallway, lurched to the front door and fumbled with the handle. Outside, it was dark and cold but the air was fresh. He leant unsteadily against the wall, taking deep breaths. The stars were very bright and he stared up at them trying to focus on them and control the spinning feeling. He shivered as the cold clamped on to his damp body but he couldn't move for fear of falling over. The top part of his body seemed heavy, and he felt an overpowering desire to let his head slump forward, but when he gave into it and closed his eyes, the spinning increased, and he wanted to be sick. He jerked his head up again and stood staring out across the street, fighting the nausea.

The music started again from inside the house and he tried

to keep his attention on the sound, forcing himself to attempt to remember the name of the group playing – but he just couldn't think of it. He knew that he ought to go back inside but the thought of the heat and the smell was too terrible. He pushed himself away from the wall and began to walk down the short path towards the road. He crashed into the gate and then couldn't find the latch to open it. Finally he gave up and stepped over the low wall, bumping his shin on it despite his effort not to. He walked along the pavement, breathing deeply and keeping his eyes fixed firmly on the lamp-post at the end of the road.

He was walking mechanically and he was terribly cold and his teeth were chattering but all the time he was moving, he could feel that he was keeping the sickness at bay. When he became aware of where he was he realized that he had walked for about three blocks, and was nearing the edge of the estate, but he kept going, determined to walk off the effects of the wine. His face felt tight and he knew that he must be very pale. Finally, as he reached the yellow glare of the main road, he turned back.

He was still very drunk and his mind was filled with random thoughts which seemed to float round his head. He tried to walk in a straight line and became aware of the cracks in the pavement. A line, then space, then a line, then space. He willed himself to keep his feet going accurately from one paving-stone to the next, but he kept missing, and he knew that he must be stumbling about wildly. Still, he no longer felt sick. The streets were empty and quiet – not even a car had passed him. A good job because if someone saw him swaying crazily along the road they might call the police and then ... He tripped over an uneven paving-stone and only saved himself from falling by grabbing on to a hedge at the edge of someone's garden. He felt a branch rip away in his grasp and he peered stupidly at the small leaves in his fist. He opened his hand and let them fall, though one stuck to the inside of his palm and he had to scrape it off. He must still be sweating. He couldn't hold

Anna's hand if his was sweaty. Anna, he thought. He must get back – she would be wondering where he was, and besides he was freezing. If he kept going he would be fine by the time he got back to the house.

Again he concentrated on the lines and spaces in front of him, sometimes looking up and checking where he was. Two streets away, then one. And finally he was back in Chris's road and he started breathing deeply again and held his head up level. He increased his pace and listened to the click of his footsteps as he walked quickly. The lamps in the road jogged up and down with every step and swayed slightly. Now he could hear the thump of the music from the party. As he neared the house, a group of people came out of the gate and walked off down the road. Leaving already? He looked at his watch. 11.30? It couldn't be. But it was. He ought to go straight in, get his coat, and go home.

He drew level with the gate and stared at the house. The front-room window was open, and he could hear the chatter of people as the music stopped again. He couldn't go home yet – he had to go back inside and see Anna. He closed his eyes and raised his finger and touched his nose. That was a test that the police used to check people's reactions when they were drunk. He passed it – but why on earth couldn't the so-and-so police stay out of his thoughts when he was trying to have fun? After all it was a great party – two Firsts, first time drunk and first time properly with a girl. Supposing she had gone?

He opened the gate and walked up to the door. It had been left on the latch, and he screwed his eyes up against the light as it swung open and he went in.

The music had stopped when he went into the room and he was surprised to see how few people there were left – no more than about fifteen. The combination of the drink and the glare of the light made it difficult to see, and he was still peering around half blindly when an ironic cheer went up:

'He's back at last.' That was Ian's voice.

'Hey, whatcher Chopper!'

'It's the hard man!'

'Where've you been, Ray? Practising your killer tackles?'

He still couldn't see properly, but it dawned on him that most of the remaining people were members of the football team. They began yelling grim reminders about his exploits in the game. He felt suddenly terribly defensive – the shouts were drunken and good-natured jibes yet he felt so open to any hidden attack. 'Whaddya mean?' His voice was slurred, and a couple of people laughed. He still couldn't make out any faces behind the veil of lines and bright colours that floated in front of his eyes.

'Whaddya mean?' He whirled round wildly, his voice loud and aggressive.

'He's drunk!' That sounded like Paul Farmer's voice. He glared in Paul's direction and saw that he was grinning.

He tottered round to face him. 'No, I'm not. What did you mean about that tackle?' he demanded.

'What?'

'That tackle was fair. There was nothing wrong with it. It was fair, see. Even Raines said it was. So you just shut your mouth.'

'I didn't say anything. What's the matter with you?' Paul's voice was loud and Ray was aware that the rest of the room was now silent. Everybody was watching him.

'It was fair, see. You just shut up saying it wasnt.' Ray could hear the childish whine in his own voice, but he couldn't switch it off: 'Nobody says that. That's all. Nobody.' He trailed off, not knowing what to say – knowing that he was just making a fool of himself. It was still quiet, and he looked round for help. Dave was sitting in the corner with Rosie, looking embarrassed, and Ray walked unsteadily over to them and slumped down on the floor nearby. They didn't speak, but little by little the others began chatting again. Then the music was turned on again, though now it was much quieter and only serving as a background to people's talk while the party obviously wound to an end.

Ray raised his eyes after a while and looked round for Anna. She was still here, sitting on the far side of the room with Ian and Jane. She was looking straight at him, but he couldn't make out the expression on her face, especially since much of it was hidden by her hair. He wanted to go to her, but after his display of stupidity, she probably didn't want to talk to him. Dave leant forward and tapped his shoulder. 'Are you O.K.?'

'Yes.' He wanted to forget what had just happened but he couldn't be angry with Dave for reminding him.

'Are you drunk?'

'A bit.'

There was a silence, then Dave nudged him: 'What about your bird then. Who is she?'

'Anna!'

'What's she like? Any luck?'

'No, it's nothing. I just had a couple of dances, that's all.'

'Get off – she was all over you.'

'It was nothing.'

'Not much! She fancies you. She keeps looking at you. Why don't you go and chat her up?'

Ray shrugged and shook his head.

'Go on, mate. I'm telling you – you're in there.'

'I can't.'

'Why not?'

'I just can't now. Blimey, I left her alone all that time and then . . . then there was that stupid stuff when I came back in.'

'Well, that was only 'cause you were drunk. She won't mind that.'

'It wasn't because I was drunk. I'm O.K., I keep telling you.' He felt his voice rising again, and he reduced it to a mumble. 'It was because they kept on at me.' Dave didn't say anything, and Ray found himself saying, 'They called me "killer".' It was good to say it, knowing that Dave couldn't possibly understand what he really meant – it was like some sort of release.

'Ah, come on, they were just mucking you about.'

He'd fished for it, but even so it was reassuring to hear that nobody else had thought that anything had been hidden in the comments.

'Anyway, I think you ought to go and talk to her. Go on – she's probably dying to talk to you.'

'O.K. I'll see you.' Ray heaved himself up and began to cross the room but he had no intention of talking to Anna yet and he went out of the door and into the kitchen. Another drink would give him that extra courage. He sorted out a glass from the chaos of bottles and left-over food from the table and rinsed it under the tap. Then he poured himself some more wine and lemonade.

Anna was still standing next to Ian and Jane, and as he walked up to her, he marvelled at his own confidence, even cheek: 'Hi.'

'Hello.'

'I'm sorry about cutting out like that – I just felt sort of hot.' Her face showed no sign of criticism – in fact, she looked anxious.

'I've got to go,' she said, but she was sorry about it – it wasn't a brush-off. 'My father's going to pick me up.'

'When?'

'Now. Any minute.'

He drank the rest of the wine. 'Well, I'll come outside with you.'

'I'll just get my coat.'

He followed her out to the hall and watched while she searched through the pile of coats on the hall-stand. Now was the time to say something – she'd be gone soon. He felt his confidence waver as he tried to say something. She found her coat and began to put it on, buttoning it up and sweeping her hair outside her collar.

'Um – shall I give you a call?' He said it so quietly that she hadn't heard.

'Mm?'

'Shall I phone you?' Weren't there any words that wouldn't sound clumsy?

'If you like.' It was shy, but she meant it.

'What's your number?'

'It's in the book. Hartfield, Eighteen Princes Close.'

'When?' He just couldn't sound casual.

'Any time.'

'Tomorrow?'

'If you like.' She hesitated and then walked towards the door. He stepped ahead of her and opened it.

'Thanks.'

He walked down the path with her. There was a car outside with the engine running.

'He's there. I've got to go.'

'O.K. I'll phone you tomorrow.'

'Yes. Good night.' She looked at him, then opened the gate and walked to the car. There, she turned round and smiled. He wanted to call out but he just moved his hand in a half-wave as she got in. The car moved off quickly and he watched it out of sight and then turned to go back inside. As he raised his hand to push the door, he saw his watch – 12.15. He had promised to be in by 11.30. He pulled the door to and walked back to the road. He didn't really fancy going back in, anyway.

The street lights still bobbed and swayed as he walked, his feet pounding heavily on the pavement. The wine was still affecting him. He started to jog-trot, thinking that it might make it wear off, but he just felt too heavy so he slowed to a walk again and began in an odd way to enjoy the feeling of unsteadiness in his body. But he felt tired and his eyes ached and soon the thought of being able to crash into his bed and sleep dominated him. He walked in a remote way, concentrating on imagining the delicious feeling of lying in bed.

It seemed to take ages to get home, and at times he had to fight a desire to just lie down and sleep where he was. His brain felt as if it wanted to close down and he was only dimly aware of pushing himself onwards with his arms flapping by his side.

Then he was outside his house, forcing himself into a final effort to find his key, close the door, and creep up the stairs. It was very dark and quiet inside and the air of the house smelt close and almost stale. The stairs creaked despite his attempts to tread softly but he reached his room without hearing any sound from his parents' bedroom. He closed his door, struggled out of his clothes in the dark, and left them dumped on the floor as he crawled into bed. The coolness of the sheets woke him up slightly, but as he laid his head down on the pillow he felt the room begin to spin and he was being dragged down with the whirlpool. For a moment he thought that he might not be able to stand the spinning, then he relaxed and let it whirl him away into unconsciousness.

Seventeen

It was raining when he woke up. He was lying twisted up and half-out of the bed, with his face pointing towards the window. As the blur gradually cleared from his mind and his eyes, he saw the tears of water running down the window-pane, distorting the trees and houses in the distance. He lay for a couple of minutes without moving, staring at the drops that ran together and slid down the glass. A buffet of wind hurled the rain against the window, and the water on it was blasted in all directions, streaking the view out of recognition. Somehow he felt that the rain was a bad sign and he slid down beneath the covers as a chill swept along his back. His head pounded with the movement, his mouth was dry and his eyes ached. He shivered again and wrapped his arms round himself – the area round his left shoulder was icy and dead so he rubbed it vigorously. When he looked at his watch – 12.35 – he thought for a moment that it must have stopped last night, but when he held it to his ear, it was still ticking. He wasn't surprised that he'd slept so late after the party and all he'd had to drink, but why hadn't his parents woken him?

It took an enormous effort to drag himself out of bed, and he had to sit on the edge of it, holding his throbbing head. He finally reached forward and grabbed the clothes that were still scattered over the floor. He pulled on a sweater, then tried dragging on a pair of pants but it was so awkward that he stood up to get them and his jeans on. His head reeled but he managed to keep standing and he shuffled over to the wall and eased his feet into his slippers.

In the bathroom he splashed cold water over his face and

cleaned his teeth to get rid of the furry feeling in his mouth, then rubbed his face briskly on the towel. He looked grey-cheeked and dreadful but he went downstairs and into the kitchen. It was warm there and when he opened the oven door he saw that there was a chicken cooking. He drank a glass of water and then poured some more to help him to swallow an aspirin that he shook from the bottle.

Derek was alone in the front room sitting on the floor next to the electric fire – he was already watching the television – a programme for farmers.

'Where are Mum and Dad?'

'Gone out.'

'Where?'

'Grandma's.'

'Why didn't they wake me up?'

'I don't know. They said to leave you.'

Had they heard him last night? Did they realize that he'd been drunk?

'Were they angry?'

'What for?'

'I don't know. Nothing.'

It was easy with Derek – he never seemed to notice anything strange about questions like that. If only other people could be asked things so directly without any suspicion. Already the boy had forgotten the question and the answer and was back in the world of farming problems.

'What time did they go out?'

'Dunno.'

'Did they leave any messages or anything?'

'No.'

'About the chicken or anything?'

'No.'

'Are we supposed to cook anything else before they come back?'

'Dunno.'

'You're very chatty today.'

Derek ignored him and continued to stare at the screen. Ray kicked Derek's foot: 'Move over,' and sat on the edge of the sofa leaning towards the fire. What time would they be home? It must be soon – the chicken looked almost cooked. Even if they got home soon, it would still be nearly two o'clock before lunch was finished. That wouldn't give him long to get to the station and catch a train to somewhere in order to post the letter. It would have to be almost the first train that came along – he could only hope that it went just far enough to get back home by about six. And the rain. That was a problem. He could hardly say he was going out to play football. After all those fine days, it would suddenly be wet – and there was something about it that seemed so wrong, almost threatening.

He got up and walked over to the window. Not only wet but blustery. The rain was being blown along the road in sheets. The heavy sky seemed to glower over the house in an unbroken mass of grey.

The family car appeared at the corner and drew into the kerb in front of the garden gate. The windscreen wipers stopped, and first his mother, then his father got out and hurried up the path to the door. Neither of them noticed him at the window.

'They're back,' he said to Derek and went out into the hall to meet them. They were both standing just inside the front door, shaking their coats.

'Hello. How is she?'

His mother looked up. 'Oh, you're up then.'

Was that meant to be a criticism or not – he couldn't tell, but decided to keep to the original subject. 'Is she O.K.? Any better?'

'Not very well.' She walked past him into the kitchen.

His father shook his head and said in a low voice. 'She's a bit poorly – don't say much to your mum – she's upset. How are you? Did you have a good time last night?'

'Great.'

'What time did you get back?'

'Oh, a bit late actually – about twelvish.'

'Well, don't say anything to your mum.'

Ray followed him to the kitchen and stood uneasily in the doorway watching while his mother took some peas out of the fridge and put them on to cook. All her movements seemed jerky and he could sense the tension as she moved about. His father seemed to be tiptoeing round the table as he laid the knives and forks – he wasn't actually tiptoeing but it really was as though he was treading warily.

Ray turned quietly and went upstairs – he'd better get ready now so that he could get out of the house as quickly as possible and with the minimum of fuss as soon as lunch was over. He went into the bathroom, peeled off his sweater, and began to wash himself properly. When his face was covered with soap he looked closely at himself and then on an impulse he took his father's razor out of the rack and drew it slowly and carefully down from his ear, along the chin to the middle. He paused for a moment to look at the soap-free strip it left, then did the same on the other side and then under his chin down towards his neck. It took less than a minute to do and then it was finished – all without a single cut. His straggly fluff had gone.

He rinsed the razor and thought about his crazy desire to kill himself on the Thursday evening. What a ridiculous idea that had been. He had survived – nothing was worth that – there was always hope. He rinsed his face and neck, dried himself and went into his room to dress. It took him ages to find a clean pair of socks and he had only just finished getting ready when his mother called out that the food was on the table. He quickly got the letter out from under the sweaters in the drawer and left it on the table so that he could just grab it and go after he'd eaten. As he left the room, he hesitated and almost went back to hide it again but then after yesterday Derek certainly wouldn't touch anything and his parents rarely went into his room so it would be safe.

The meal was waiting, but only his mother was in the kitchen. 'Shall I go and call Dad and Derek?'

'No, it's all right – your Dad's just nipped down for some beer, and Derek will be in in a minute.' She paused, then sat down and looked directly at him. Her eyes had dark rings round them and there was a suspicion of tears – they had been looking like that for a couple of days now. 'Ray, I want you to do me a favour. I know you think that Derek ought to know about Grandma but I do think he's too young. Look, someone must go and see her again this afternoon, and I think that if me and your Dad go, Derek'll start asking questions. And anyway I don't want to worry your grandma – she'll think it's strange if we keep rushing in to see her.' She stopped for a moment, and he looked away from her as he realized with a terrible certainty what she was going to ask. With his mind already swinging round with the possibilities he heard her ask, 'So do you think you could go and see her? She'd love that – it would really cheer her up a lot.'

Some excuses hovered on the tip of his tongue but he glanced at her strained face and managed to say, 'O.K.'

Her eyes brightened. 'Oh, thanks, Ray – that's really good of you. I expect Dad'll take . . . Here comes Derek, don't say anything about it.'

She got up and pretended to be doing something at the stove as Derek came in and sat down. Her voice sounded very false to Ray as she turned round with a smile on her face. 'Come on, you two, you may as well start, Dad'll be back in a minute. Serve him right if it's cold – I told him only five minutes.' She sat down and started to eat. 'What did you do this morning, Derek?' Her voice was jolly, but Ray had noticed that dig at his father – she really was in a mood.

'Nothing.'

The conversation ceased, and in the awkward silence Ray forced himself to pick up his knife and fork and start to eat. He heard the front door bang and his mother said in a voice that betrayed her relief at being able to say something:

'Oh, he's back.'

His father was soaking wet, and his hair was plastered down on his forehead, dripping with rain.

'That stinking car!' He began to pull off the thick white sweater he was wearing. It was drenched and drops fell from it as he pulled it over his head. 'Oh – it's sopping. Honestly, that car! A drop of water and the wretched thing won't start.'

'What's the matter with it, Bob?'

'Ah, nothing much – it's just got some water on the electrics, that's all – but I can't get it to start and there's no hope of drying it off in this weather. I tried but the stupid thing just got even wetter and so did I.'

'Didn't you get the beer, then?'

'No,' he snapped, rubbing his hair with a towel. 'I've been all this time trying to dry the beastly thing off. Honestly, the people that design these cars ought to flipping well have to drive them for a while. But I expect they all drive around in Rolls-Royces. It's just badly designed. I mean, I know it's wet, but blimey you expect a car to be able to go in a bit of rain.'

'Well, come and eat your dinner – it'll warm you up.'

His father sat down and continued to grumble, but Ray wasn't listening. What was he going to do about the letter? There would be no chance of going to the hospital and then catching a train. He'd probably only have about an hour to spare and he could get nowhere in that time. Could it wait? The next opportunity to post it wouldn't be for another week – next Sunday, in fact – that is, if he was picked to play football again next Saturday and surely he would be. He simply couldn't go after school on a weekday – there'd never be enough time. That meant it would have to wait – a whole week! And during that time the police would continue their investigations and they'd be looking for a young person living in the area, whereas the letter might have sent them off into another direction altogether. Could he change his mind – tell his mother that he'd forgotten, that he'd arranged to do something? Perhaps he could object to going out in all this rain – especially now that Dad couldn't take him to the hospital. But of course if the rain stopped him from going to the hospital, it would stop him from going out anywhere. Oh, why ever did she have to ask today?

'Hurry up, Ray – we've all finished, and I want to go and watch the telly.'

'Blimey, Derek, can't you wait?' he asked.

'No.'

'That's all right, Derek. You go and watch it – I'll bring your pudding in.'

The young boy could hardly believe his ears and he looked quizzically at his mother. 'Really?'

'Yes, off you go.'

He got up and rushed out before she changed her mind.

'What's that for?' asked his father, surprised and slightly irritated.

'Nothing. Well, he's not had much the last couple of days, with us being out all the time.'

'I can't eat any more, Mum.' Ray pushed his plate towards her as she cleared away.

'Well, there's only apricots for pudding.'

'I'm not hungry.'

It was true, the change in plan had left him feeling worried and had taken his appetite away.

'Are you going to the hospital, Ray?'

'Yes.'

'Well, I'm afraid I won't be able to run you in in the car.'

His mother turned from the draining-board and her voice was snappy and hard. 'Why not?'

And his father's voice too was irritable when he replied, 'Haven't you been listening? I can't get the so-and-so thing to go!'

'Can't you dry it out?'

'Oh for Pete's sake, don't be stupid! I can't dry it when it's pouring with rain – it's teeming outside.'

His father so rarely lost his temper, even mildly, that it always shocked Ray when he did and he sat now feeling embarrassed at this sudden burst between them.

His mother banged down the tin of apricots. 'Well, there's no need to talk to me like that.'

'Well, you act as if it was my fault.'

'I said nothing of the sort!'

Ray cut in quickly, standing up: 'Look, it's O.K. I'll go on the bus.' It would be so easy to exploit the situation and claim that he couldn't go now that he wasn't getting a lift, but he couldn't stand it when there was a row – especially if he was connected in any way. His father had been going to say something else but Ray saw him make the effort and instead he sat staring at the table. His mother was still glaring, her face taut and angry.

'Honestly – it's O.K. I'll go on the bus. It's no problem.' He tried to make his voice calmer.

The whole situation – the rain, the ruined plans and this unexpected explosion of tension from his parents – was boiling inside Ray, and the fear that he had beaten away in the last couple of days was suddenly weighing him down again. Now he just wanted to get out of the house and have time to sort things out. 'There's a city bus at quarter to two – I'll make it if I run.'

His father fumbled in his pocket and brought out his wallet. 'Look, take some money.'

'It's O.K. I've got some.'

'No, please.' He pushed a pound-note towards Ray. It was a token – a sort of apology – so he took it.

'I'll give you the change when I get back.'

His parents were both standing still like wax-works. Ray looked at them for a moment, then he rushed upstairs, grabbed his parka off the chair and ran down and out of the door.

The rain beat on to him even in the shelter of the doorway as he stood pulling the parka on. He raised the hood and then dashed down the path and out into the road trying to put the zip together as he ran. He kept his head down and fumbled with the zip but it was slowing him down so he just held the parka together and increased his speed.

When he reached the main road, he saw that the bus wasn't in sight, so he slackened his pace and kept close into the shop fronts to keep drier. He stopped, panting, in a doorway opposite the bus-stop.

It was good to be out – the cold, and even the rain, seemed better than the atmosphere in the kitchen. What the hell was the matter with them both? His mother could often be short-tempered, but usually his father could ride it and calm things down. But today – it was almost as if they wanted to shout at each other. It was probably the strain of the hospital and his grandmother's illness, but even so. He was well out of it – even in this dreadful weather. The gutters were nearly overflowing with water, and the nearest drain was blocked, forming a huge puddle out in the road. There was no one in sight, and only a couple of cars passed in the five minutes before he saw the bus coming in the distance. He stayed in the shelter as long as possible, then ducked out and held his arm out to stop it.

Ray went and sat up in the front seat behind the driver. He paid his fare and then settled down to watch the road ahead. The rain was heavier than ever, and the driver was keeping well out of the side of the road to avoid the puddles but despite this, the bus still sent jets of spray shooting out, and Ray leant against the window to watch it.

The thought of the hospital began to nag at him. He hated the smell of hospitals, and he dreaded seeing all the old and ill people there. What would he talk about to his grandmother? It would be awkward to talk about her illness, and he could hardly tell her about what he had been doing for the last couple of days. He could ramble on about the football match for a while and then maybe tell her about the party. For the first time he looked back at the previous evening and remembered Anna. It all seemed so remote. Had she liked him, or was it just what he had imagined because of the drink? Well, she'd given him her address and said he could ring. What was it? He couldn't remember. He screwed up his eyes and tried to recall the moment, trying to hear her saying it – something Princes Close. What was the number? And what was her surname? His mind remained blank and he wrestled with it to try and re- member – Anna . . . Hartfield – that was it. Hartfield, Princes Close. The number didn't matter – he could look it up in the phone-book, there wouldn't be more than one family of that name in that street. He'd look it up and phone her when he got out of the hospital.

There was something else, too, at the back of his mind, but he just couldn't remember what. Even the streets of the city were empty – no one walking and only a few cars. He got up and rang the bell as they passed the bus-stop before the Central Hospital and he began to walk down the aisle. The only other passenger, an old man wearing a hat and carrying an um- brella, was getting off here too, and Ray waited for him to walk unsteadily along the bus, gripping on tight to each seat as he went. The bus slowed and stopped outside the hospital and the man stepped carefully down on to the pavement – first one foot and then the other. Ray jumped off from the other side of the white pole on the platform and as he did so, he saw himself running down the stairs out of the house, jumping the last three steps in his hurry. And the memory that he had been searching for came bursting on him – the letter – he had left the letter to the police on the table by the side of his bed.

Eighteen

The first rush of panic almost knocked him to the ground, his mind bouncing erratically from one terrible possibility to another. Then the calm, plotting part of him came into play. So calm, so plotting that a bit of him seemed to stand outside and watch, disgusted at the way he worked coolly through the facts and prepared to cope.

There would be no bus home for another hour, so he couldn't get back and hide it; besides, that would look suspicious and all kinds of awkward questions would be asked. Actually it was fairly safe where he'd left it. Derek wouldn't go to his room and touch anything, and the chances were very low that either of his parents would, either. So all the panic was stupid. Besides, the letter was sealed. Even if they did see it, they would never open it, and he could easily lie his way out of the address — say he'd found it, say he was holding it for some other boy ... Oh, how easily all those plausible lies and excuses rolled off his mind!

Some water ran down the back of his neck, reminding him that he was standing in the middle of the pavement getting drenched. He pulled the hood over his head and walked through the main gates and along the road to the hospital. He headed towards the middle one of the three main buildings. The dirty, dark brown brickwork and the small windows were depressing and gloomy, especially in the grey wetness of the day, and Ray steeled himself to face the grim corridors and hospital smell inside.

At the inquiries desk, he asked the attendant where he would find his grandmother, then followed the instructions up two flights of stairs and along a drably painted corridor to the ward. He was early. With two other people he waited outside the double swing doors, peering through the glass to look for his grandmother. Most of the beds were obscured by green curtains hanging from ugly rails that projected from the walls. The room was large and high and lit by harsh neon ceiling strips, and the only relief was a long, highly polished table down the centre of the floor on which were two vases of flowers – but even these looked limp as though overcome by the disinfectant and germs in the air. Two nurses bustled in and out of the various cubicles formed by the curtains – probably tidying the patients up before visiting hours. Ray felt beads of sweat break out above his upper lip – due partly to the stuffiness of the building but also because of the tension and distaste that pressed down on him.

A clock on the far wall of the ward worked its way methodically towards half-past two. How long would he have to stay? At least the full visiting-time, probably about one hour. After all, if he found it unpleasant there, it must be far worse for his grandmother to have to lie there, hour after hour for days or perhaps even weeks. He must try and cheer her up and tell her lots of news and keep her mind off her illness – whatever it was. Did she know what it was? Did his parents? He didn't even know what part of her body was affected – but he could hardly ask her.

There were now nearly a dozen people waiting outside the doors, some of them carrying flowers or small packets. He should have brought her something, but it hadn't occurred to him before.

A nurse pulled open the doors and locked them back against the wall, and the other visitors began to push past him into the ward. They were nearly all inside before he forced himself to join them. He walked down the centre aisle, looking nervously left and right at the beds. All the patients were old and his stomach tightened as he thought suddenly that they looked like people who had been put there to die.

By the time he had reached the end of the aisle he had still not seen his grandmother and he thought for a moment that he had come to the wrong ward. He walked back up the aisle and in the bed nearest the door he saw her. He realized how he'd managed to walk past her, for even the worst that he had been expecting was not as bad as the reality. She was almost unrecognizable. She had always been such a lively woman, and to see her lying back on the pillow, with her grey hair straight and straggly about her white face, filled him with dread. Her hands were clutching the sheets tightly and her eyes were closed. For a moment he wanted to walk away quickly before she saw him, but he pushed the thought out of his mind and moved quietly towards the bed, and sat down on the wooden chair next to it. She still didn't open her eyes, and he leant towards her and said gently, 'Grandma.'

Her eyes remained closed. Was she asleep? Ought he to leave her alone? He looked around, but the curtains that hung on either side of the bed allowed him to see only across the room to the patient opposite. Should he get up and go and ask a nurse? He turned back to her and almost whispered, 'Grandma, it's Ray.'

Her eyes flickered and then opened and she rolled her head towards him. It seemed to take her a long time to recognize him, but then she smiled and looked immediately much more like the person he knew.

'Ray.' Her voice was absolutely normal – he'd always liked it, with its distinct Midlands accent much stronger than his or his family's. 'How are you?'

The strength of her voice gave him hope, and he laughed and said, 'I'm fine. How are you?'

'Sleepy. They keep giving me tablets, and they make me sleepy.'

Although his initial shock had worn off, he felt awkward and uncertain what to say, and she was obviously in a drugged state and unable to hold a conversation. But he was determined that he was going to make it as easy as possible for them both.

'Well, don't worry about that – you just be still, and I'll talk.' That was the hardest part over, and now that he had made up his mind what he was going to do, he started to talk. Anything would do. He told her about the weather, the journey to the hospital, the football match, what had happened at school, the practice matches, programmes he'd seen on TV. Stupid stories and boring bits of information poured out of him. He described everything in great detail, and he didn't stop to think what he was talking about. She just lay and looked at him, occasionally smiling and nodding her head, but mostly just looking directly at his face. Sometimes he would catch her gaze, but more often he talked with his eyes focused on the pillow just behind her head. He knew that much of what he was saying was ridiculous and trivial, but he was suddenly painfully aware of what she needed – just to listen, just to have someone tell her about things and take her mind off herself.

He knew this, he realized, because that was what he would want if he was in the same position – in fact, it was what he had wanted from people a couple of times during the past few days. And the talking was easy. Only half his brain was needed – and the other half was filled with pictures and thoughts of what had been happening to him. He was aware of them but they were never allowed to come together in a proper sequence as he chatted on, trying to keep her entertained.

For a moment he thought that he had exhausted everything, but he suddenly remembered the party, and he began to tell her all about it – even the bits about getting drunk and meeting Anna. As he talked about Anna, he could see her clearly, and he was seized with a desire to meet her again. He must telephone her as soon as he got out of here. And then he heard his grandmother talking.

'Ray, you *are* wicked. Fancy getting drunk at your age.' She laughed. 'If your mother found out.' This was his grandmother again. Despite the pale skin and straggly hair, he saw her as she had always been to him – someone he could tell things to, who would understand, discuss, even criticize, but always someone whose criticism was underlined with a belief in him.

For a moment he considered saying what was really on his mind, but then even she would be horrified. Besides she was in no state to help him.

The chuckle faded from her voice. 'Oh, I'm so tired,' she said. She closed her eyes and began breathing hard. It wasn't tiredness – it was pain. As he watched her hands clench, he felt again his inadequacy to help her. But after a bit the pain seemed to pass, and he could see her relax. She lay still and appeared to be asleep again. He sat for a couple of minutes, then slowly got up and walked to the end of the bed and looked round the curtains. Perhaps he ought to tell a nurse about her – but there was no one in sight. He glanced at the clock – nearly 3.20 – the time had shot past.

'Ray – don't go.' She had woken up again, and she was stretching out her hand towards him.

'I wasn't. I was just checking the time.' He moved back to her and touched her hand. She wanted to hold his, he knew, but he just touched her and then took his hand away, pretending to pull up the chair. Some terrible fear kept him away from that simple gesture – almost as if her illness could be passed on to him. He loved her so much, and yet her condition repelled him.

'How's your mother?' she said, and her voice was now quieter and less lively – as though she had been drained by the spasm of pain.

'Oh – she's . . . she's O.K. A bit sort of . . .' He shouldn't tell her about the tension and anxiety that his mother was obviously going through. 'A bit tired, I suppose.'

'She's worried about me.' Her voice was very quiet now.

'No.' He tried to sound bright and cheerful.

'That's her trouble.'

'No, she's fine.'

'She can't accept things.'

He found that he couldn't say anything. His grandmother's

eyes were closed again, and she looked shrunken and frail as she had done when he had arrived.

'She thinks she can change things – that's why she worries. But she can't.' Her voice was almost a whisper now, and he felt that he ought not to listen – she was just talking without realizing what she was saying. 'Nobody can. You just have to get used to it. She thinks I'm dying, and even if I am, she can't do anything about it.'

He squirmed away from listening, and yet he felt compelled to stay and hear it. She was dying, then, and she knew it.

'She doesn't realize.'

He must go – it was disgusting, staying here and listening. She didn't know what she was saying.

'She's more worried about it than I am. But you learn, you see.' Her mind wandered away, and she stopped, and her eyes creased as another wave of pain began. But it was short, and her face relaxed again, and she turned and looked directly at him, and he saw that she hadn't been talking wildly – she had been talking to him and had meant him to hear.

'Do you understand?'

'What, Grandma?'

'She hasn't learned about life yet.'

'What do you mean?' If she was talking to him, then he could find out what she meant.

'She tries to avoid things all the time – and it's no good. You can't. They'll happen anyway. The only way you can ever be happy is to accept it. If you try and run away from what's going to happen it doesn't stop it from happening. Do you see?'

He did, in a way, but the room seemed so close and the air so stale that he just had to go.

'Yes. Well, I'd better go now – it's time to go now, Grandma.' He stood up. Her eyes held his, though.

'It's important, Ray.'

'Yes, I know, Grandma. I understand.' He would faint if he didn't get out. 'I've got to go – I'll see you soon. Look after yourself. 'Bye.' He would, he would force himself to bend down and kiss her good-bye, but she had closed her eyes again and obviously wasn't expecting him to do anything. He brushed her hand lightly with his.

'See you,' he said and then walked quickly away and out of the ward.

He stopped for a moment outside the swing doors, but the heat and the smell still clung to him there, so he walked along the corridor and down the stairs. The air got cooler and fresher, and by the time he reached the main foyer, he felt he could breathe again. Outside, it was still raining, though less heavily. There was a black car standing at the bottom of the steps to the building and the engine was running and the wind-screen wipers were slapping backwards and forwards but there was nobody inside. Beyond it, across the courtyard, was a small building with a steep V-shaped roof and a tall chimney, belching what could have been smoke or steam. For a moment he wondered if it was some sort of crematorium and he pictured somebody inside burning all the organs and limbs that had been removed in operations. Then he saw a man open the door and pull out a large wicker trolley, and realized that it must be the hospital laundry.

It was just past 3.30 and he could hear the bell ringing to announce the end of visiting hours. There wouldn't be a bus for another twenty minutes. He had just time enough to phone Anna. He want back inside to the telephone-box by the stair-case. Seeing someone in there, he sat down on a long wooden bench to wait. Directly in front of him was the bust of a man, with a brass plate below it – 'Gordon Manson K.G. Founder of Central Hospital.' On the right of the bust, on the wall, was a photograph of a group of people standing in front of a hospital van. He got up and walked closer to look at the photograph. There was an inscription below it – 'Hospital Bus. Presented by the Friends of Central Hospital, 1967.' Standing in the middle of the group, wearing a large flowery hat, was Mrs Chalmers.

For nearly a minute Ray stood staring at her face. He was

not scared or shocked, not even surprised. It was almost as if he had known that she might be there, and his mind coped with it logically and coolly. After all, she had been a hospital worker – he had known that since the newspaper report on Friday. Besides, since the accident his whole life had been narrowed down to thoughts about it and it seemed almost natural that everything that happened was connected in some way. And now there she was smiling out towards him and he felt nothing except a slight unease at the inevitability of it. When he stepped backwards and pretended to look closely at the bust he was aware that he was play-acting out of habit. He was defending himself by not allowing anybody to see him looking too closely at the photograph and perhaps linking him with her death, but he was doing it almost without really caring whether anybody saw him or not.

The phone-box was empty now. He walked casually away from the photograph and into the booth, he laid the book across the coin box and thumbed through for the 'H's. He found the address – Hartfield, 18 Princes Close – and memorized the number, got out a ten-piece coin, and dialled. The phone was answered almost immediately by a man.

'Can I speak to Anna, please?'

'Hold on, I'll get her.'

He heard the phone being put down, and then he began to worry about what to say – the whole thing had been done in such a hurry and he wished that he had planned it more carefully.

'Hello?' He hadn't remembered what her voice sounded like.

'Anna?'

'Yes?'

'It's Ray – from the party.'

'Hello.'

He hesitated – he felt very unsure of everything and he found that he was trying to work out what she was thinking by the tone of her voice. Perhaps she already had a boy-friend and had only been being polite when she'd said he could ring. Besides, he didn't even know what he wanted to say. The silence was awkward and he broke it with a rush.

'How are you? Did you get home O.K.?'

'Yes, thanks. Did you?'

'Yes.'

'I didn't think you would.'

The reminder about his drunken state confused him even more. He now knew what he wanted to say, but he couldn't get the words out. Supposing he asked her out for a date and she said no. It had been so easy last night with the wine but today, on the phone, not sure of what she was thinking, he couldn't do it.

'No. I was all right. I left straight after you did.'

She made a non-committal sound at the other end of the line, and the last ounce of courage left him.

'Anyway, I thought I'd look up your number to see if I could find it. So I'll ring you sometime, O.K.? Well, I've got to go now, or I'll miss the bus. I'll see you.'

'O.K. 'Bye.' She put down the phone, and he stood for a moment listening to the silence before he slammed the receiver down and pushed open the door. He had really messed that up. What a stupid thing to do. He should have waited until he had worked out something to say. Now it would be almost impossible to ring again. He crossed the foyer and went out of the main exit and down the steps, pulling his hood up as the rain beat on to him.

Nineteen

There were over a dozen people waiting for the bus – most of them had obviously just come from the hospital because apart from them the street was deserted. They were huddled against the wall sheltering from the rain. Ray joined them. The guttering above must have been blocked, for it was sending down a steady stream of water, which bounced off the pavement, occasionally spraying people's shoes and lower legs, but it was a lot less wet under there than standing out near the bus-stop.

He was still angry with himself for having messed up the phone-call to Anna, and he was thinking that he ought to ring her again and try to make a better impression when he noticed the waiting group surge towards the edge of the pavement. He forgot the falling water and suddenly felt a pounding on his hood as he walked through it. He jerked the hood back off his head to shake the water off before it soaked through. At the same time as the bus began to slow and pull into the kerb, he saw the number 53 on the front. In that same moment, a voice said, 'Oh hello, Ray. What are you doing here?'

It was Dave's mother.

'Oh, hello, Mrs Fitzroy.'

The bus had stopped and was towering over them, rattling and chugging. The queue edged forward to get on, taking Ray with it. A number 53 bus. He knew with a numbing certainty that he had been on this bus before. And the conductor, whom he had glimpsed through the window, was the same one who had seen him last Wednesday night.

Somehow Mrs Fitzroy had got behind him, and as he hesitated at the boarding platform, he felt her hand press him forward. 'Come on, Ray, this is ours.'

He hung back, groping wildly for some excuse to prevent him getting on, but the bell rang and the engine increased its impatient rumble and his legs carried him upwards on to the platform, and he felt Mrs Fitzroy clamber on behind. The bus began to move. He turned towards the stairs, but she caught hold of his arm.

'Let's go downstairs. I don't like the smoke.' Again he felt her hand guide him, and he ducked his head and began to walk along the aisle.

'This'll do,' she said and he turned back and sat beside her – the less fuss he made, the less obvious he was, the better. As he settled, he kept his face bent low, aware of the conductor walking towards them. He brushed past, and, noticing things with a total clarity, Ray saw the dark blue uniform that he was wearing and noted the heaviness and thickness of the material. He heard him clumping up the stairs, and he wondered, absurdly, if he was wearing heavy boots too.

Mrs Fitzroy was opening the bag which she had on her lap, and Ray felt in his pocket for his fare. If he had the right change, he could just hand it to the conductor without looking up. Yes, he had a ten and a two pence piece. He glanced at Mrs Fitzroy and saw to his dismay that she was taking out a pound-note from her purse. That would mean a delay while she got her change – plenty of chance for him to be recognized. Could he offer to pay her fare? It would seem strange but anything was better than being seen.

His voice was shaking: 'Is that all you've got? I've got the right money, I think.' He fumbled in his pocket again.

'No, it's all right, dear, I want to get some change for the meter anyway.'

It was no use arguing. He must try and calm down, stop shaking. Could he get off? Say he had to visit someone? Say he was sick?

'I didn't see you there, Ray. Have you been to the hospital?'

145

'Yes!' Was that the conductor coming down the stairs again? He daren't look round. If it was, he couldn't possibly walk down and pay his fare and get off. His only chance was to sit tight and keep his head down. Even if he was delayed having to give change to Mrs Fitzroy, the conductor would only see the top of his head and there would be no chance of recognizing him like that – the only danger would be if he saw his face. The memory of that moment last Wednesday when the conductor had grabbed his arm and looked directly in his face had haunted him so badly that he had tried to forget it. If there had been one fatal chance, it had been that one. This man, who was now either still upstairs or standing on the platform where the incident had happened, was the one person who could destroy him.

'Who were you visiting, Ray?'

'My grandmother.'

'Oh, dear. What's the matter with her?'

'I don't know.'

'How long has she been ill?'

'A couple of days.'

Of course, there were a lot of things that he didn't know. All the time he had been wondering about the police and had been trying to work out what they had found out and how they were investigating the accident – even then he had never fully believed in it. They had never been real to him. Those people who were thinking and planning, questioning and guessing, all to find him out, to bring him out into the light in order to punish him.

'Is she very old?'

'About sixty-five.'

'Oh, not all that old, then.'

'No.'

'I've been visiting my sister – she's just had an operation.'

'Oh.'

'She's over it now, though. I hope she'll be out in a couple of days, poor thing.'

She raised her pound-note and turned towards the aisle and when Ray sneaked a look backwards, he saw the conductor moving along collecting fares.

'It's funny, I didn't recognize you at the bus-stop at first because you had that hood up.'

The words struck home, and his hand rose instinctively to pull the hood up. But what could he use as an excuse? He sensed the conductor just behind him – this was his last chance.

'Yes, it was the rain. I walked under a stream of water from that gutter and it soaked me. Look.' As the conductor drew level with him, he pulled the hood over his head. Now he would be completely safe. 'Twelve, please.' Keeping his face turned towards Mrs Fitzroy, he held out his money. He felt the ticket being placed in his hand. Mrs Fitzroy leant over in front of him and offered the pound-note.

'Twelve, please. Sorry I haven't got any change.' The conductor's hand slowly came down and took the note, and there was something in the slowness that made Ray's heart pound. It was as though the movements were mechanical – as though the conductor was thinking of someone else.

'Yes, it's been a terrible day, hasn't it?' Mrs Fitzroy was saying. 'I got absolutely drenched. Mind you, I was lucky because my husband took me to the hospital in the car but, of course, I couldn't expect him to wait for me.'

The bell rang, and Ray felt the conductor's body press close into him as someone pushed past them. He hadn't given Mrs Fitzroy the ticket yet, and Ray could almost feel the stare of the conductor, though he kept his head down and could only see the man's feet. He wasn't wearing boots.

And then he knew his mistake – the hood. He had been so clever all this time. He had kept one jump ahead of everyone. His brain had been so quick to think of excuses and lies. And now he had made his first mistake. Nobody would have recognized the top of his head – all he had had to do was keep calm and not let the conductor see his face. But in his desire to stay one jump ahead, to make himself safer, he had raised his hood.

And if there was one thing that the man might have remembered, apart from his face, it was that. In his effort to avoid being recognized, he had simply made himself more obvious.

Still there was no ticket, and he heard the conductor clear his voice to speak. The bus was slowing and pulling into the kerb at a stop. He felt a hand touch his shoulder.

'Excuse me. Were you . . .? Have I . . .?' He obviously did not quite know how to ask the question. The bus had stopped and was vibrating. Ray looked up slightly and saw the driver behind the glass of his cab, turning round to see why the bell hadn't been rung to signal him to move. The driver turned round again and began to accelerate as the conductor started to speak.

'Did I see you . . .?'

Ray stood up abruptly and swung his arm round, pushing the conductor aside, and ran down towards the entrance. The bus was gathering speed when he reached the platform and behind him he could hear the surprised shouts from the conductor and Mrs Fitzroy as he jumped off. He slipped as he hit the ground but kept his balance and began to run. He heard the bell being rung frantically, but he didn't look round as his feet beat along the pavement.

He ran about fifty yards and then darted across the empty road towards a turning on the far side. As he ran, he glanced back and saw that the bus had stopped and that the conductor had jumped off and started to chase him but had given up and was now standing in the rain, staring.

Ray bolted down the side road and headed towards another turning on the right. Skidding round a fence, he knocked his hand on the wood, and the pain shot up his arm, but he didn't slow until he reached another corner and turned left. This road led back to the main road but just before he reached it, there was an alleyway. He ducked down it and ran along, jumping the many puddles and ruts. This alley was an access passage to the back of the houses along the main road and a number of garages opened on to it. One door was ajar and the interior was empty. Ray glanced back along the alley. No one was there. He stepped inside and collapsed panting against the concrete wall and slid down it until he was half-sitting, half-crouching on the floor. The only sounds, when he forced himself to hold his breath, were the rain and the pounding of blood in his ears. There were no running footsteps, no shouts of pursuit. He gasped some fresh air into his lungs and allowed his body to slump fully on to the oily floor.

He lay there, collapsed, for nearly fifteen minutes, not allowing himself to think about anything else except his exhaustion, raw lungs, and throbbing hand. Then, as his pain eased, he stood up and walked round the garage. His legs were rather wobbly. He wanted to sit down, but he kept moving because he couldn't trust himself not to start thinking about . . . He pressed both his hands tight against his mouth, but the tension inside him burst, and suddenly he began to scream. It ripped the back of his throat and soon petered out into a cough, but the pressure had eased and the madness that had been beating inside his skull had been driven out by the pent-up noise he had made.

There was no point in staying inside this garage – it was gloomy and cold. Outside was better. He stepped out into the rain and walked towards the road. It had grown so dark while he had been inside that he could now hardly see to avoid puddles. He reached the end of the alley and looked quickly up and down the road. No one. He turned right and walked slowly along the brick-walled side of the house. At the main road, he hesitated and then peeped round the corner. The bus had gone and there was no sign of anyone looking for him.

He turned towards the centre of the city, strolling along and making no effort to hide from the rain.

It must have happened almost exactly as he had imagined it would. The police must have worked out that whoever had been riding the bike had then gone down to the main road and either hitched a lift or caught a bus. They would have contacted the bus company and interviewed the drivers and conductors who had passed there at around that time, and, of course, they would have heard about 'John Timpson'. How obvious and clumsy he had been that night – getting on at the bus-stop nearest to Blackston Road immediately after the accident, having no money. The conductor would have remembered him instantly and when the police found 'Timpson's' name and address were false, they would have known they were on the right track. But then what would they have done? Got some Identikit drawings made from the conductor's description and scoured the whole city – inquiring at schools, youth clubs, cafés, everywhere. And eventually somebody would probably have recognized him, and they would have traced him.

But none of that was necessary now. He had made it easy for them. Like a blundering amateur he had gone straight to the only witness and as good as shouted, 'You don't remember me, do you?' Of course, there was always the chance that someone would see him unless he had spent the next couple of years hiding in his bedroom. And even then, with a good description of him, it was only a question of time before the police had caught up.

Now what? The conductor would have got back on to the bus and immediately questioned Mrs Fitzroy, and she would have told him everything – name, address, telephone number. So now it was just a question of time – whether he stopped the bus at the next phone-box and rang the police straight away, or whether he waited until he got to the bus-station before he rang. Then? Would the police go round to his house at once? It was Sunday, but Sundays were just as good as any other days on which to arrest somebody. They might be heading towards his house at this very moment, and at the very most it could only be about four hours before there was a knock at the door and his parents found out the whole truth about him. It would be easier that way – he couldn't possibly begin to explain it all himself. This way all he had to do was admit that it was true and hope that the police took him away before there was time for all the tears and questions, and those terrible silences and searching looks.

The thought of facing his parents and of seeing the misery that he would cause them brought him up short. Wasn't there some way out, some way of escaping the destruction of himself and his family? Supposing he just denied everything? The conductor would identify him, but that was just one man's word against another's. The conductor had made a mistake: Ray had not been on that bus on Wednesday night, he had been at home on that evening — his parents could testify that he'd only been out for twenty minutes. Could it work? Could he brazen it out somehow and simply continue to say that they were mistaking him for somebody else? After all, he didn't look wildly different from hundreds of boys of his age. He had no real distinguishing marks. His clothes were not unusual — even the parka that had given him away: most of the people he knew had ones exactly like his.

The thoughts were racing now. Things weren't so finished — there was still hope.

Perhaps he could even turn the parka to his advantage by suggesting that the conductor had only recognized it, not him.

It could be done — all he had to do was keep denying what the conductor said and hinting that a mistake had been made. If he was careful and clever the police might suspect him but they couldn't prove anything. Their whole case would rest on the one, rather doubtful, identification.

But then why had he behaved so guiltily on the bus? Why had he jumped off and run away if he had been innocent of any crime?

His heart lurched. If only he had stayed on the bus, sat tight and acted as if he didn't understand what the man was saying. But it was no good playing that 'if only' game — he was finished with games. He had to be cool and clever and work things out cunningly — no more games, no more shame at how easily he lied.

All right, why had he jumped off the bus so suddenly? He had felt sick? He had suddenly remembered something that he had lost? Possibly, but they were too simple and obvious to carry the ring of truth. It had to be something more dramatic than that. His grandmother? He couldn't use her surely? But why not? He had been worried about her during the visit . . . Mrs Fitzroy had asked him about her . . . and then suddenly he had had a flash, a warning, that she was about to die. So he had jumped off the bus to go back to see her. Then after a while he had realized that he was just being stupid and that she was probably perfectly well. Perhaps he could even go back to the hospital and ask about her – make sure that he was seen by somebody who could confirm his alibi.

That was good, very good. They would still suspect him, but the story would be plausible, and if he actually did go to the hospital, it would at least be half true.

He came out of his thoughts and realized that he was standing stock still in the middle of the pavement in the pouring rain. His clothes were completely soaked and he could feel the dampness against his skin. During his frenzied thinking he had walked without noticing where he was going, and he was now nearly back at the hospital. That must be a sign, as though he had been led there. This plan *would* work.

He broke into a run and turned in through the hospital gates, along the drive and up the stairs. Inside, he was suddenly conscious of how bedraggled he must look. Well, that would make it certain that he would be remembered.

He approached the attendant at the inquiries desk. 'Excuse me. I came here to visit my grandmother this afternoon, and then when I was on my way home, I suddenly had the feeling that she . . . that something had happened to her. So I came back to find out if she's all right. Do you think you could help me?'

He must have done it well, because the attendant smiled sympathetically and said, 'Yes, of course. What's her name?'

As he gave the man the information, Ray felt a buzzing begin in his head. The man turned away and picked up a phone, and Ray walked towards a bench and sat down, swamped with horror. What had he done? Supposing the lie came true and she was dead? He felt the skin burning on his face. It would be his fault, his lies and frantic concern for self-protection would have killed her, just as his stealing the motor-bike had killed Mrs Chalmers. You just couldn't use things like that without them swinging round and paying you back. Somehow a lie as terrible as his would bring its own horrific reward. He would have two deaths on his hands. He shouldn't have done it.

The man had put down the phone and was calling him over. She was dead. He had killed her with his lies.

'There's nothing to worry about. The nurse has had a look at her and says she's quite comfortable. So don't worry. You can go home – and I'd get out of those clothes if I were you, you're soaked through.'

'Thanks. Thanks very much. I will.'

Outside he shook his head and wanted to burst out of himself. The fever in his brain was making it difficult to see straight. He had to rest – sleep. Yet he couldn't go home yet. He needed time to pull himself together, let things work themselves out and then face whatever was going to happen with a clearer mind. There was just one further thing to do and then he would go somewhere and relax for a bit. The cinema. It would be warm and dark in there and he could lose himself for a time.

He walked on towards the nearest cinema. There was a telephone-box just outside it, and he steeled himself for one last action before he could get some peace. He dialled his home and stood listening to the ring. It was a long time before anyone answered and he felt certain that the police were already there. The pips obscured the voice at the other end and he hesitated before pushing the coin in.

'Hello.' It was Derek.

'Hi, it's Ray.'

'Oh, do you want Mum?'

'No, it's O.K. Derek, is there anybody there?'

'Who?' They hadn't arrived yet then.

'Look, can you tell Mum and Dad that I've been back to the hospital and now I'm just going to the cinema. I'll be home later.'

'O.K.'

'Don't forget – I've been back to the hospital and I'm going to the cinema.'

'Right.'

'See you.'

'Yes. 'Bye.'

He put down the phone and breathed a sigh of relief. He ought to have given them some sort of warning but that would have seemed suspicious. Anyway, he still had a bit of time to rest and work things out.

He noticed that the film poster displayed an 'X' certificate, but he walked straight in and asked for a ticket, and the cashier didn't even question him as she gave it to him with his change.

Twenty

He sat in the front row and lay back to look up at the huge screen. The film had already started as he walked down the aisle and he felt a sense of disappointment that he had missed the bit that said 'This is to certify . . .' It would have been good to see the 'X' written there and feel a thrill of daring at seeing a film that he shouldn't. Instead he caught only the last credit. 'Directed by . . .' and an Italian name. It turned out to be a cowboy picture with Clint Eastwood, and he settled back and let the action flow over him.

It was warm and comfortable in the dark, and he found himself drawn into the huge, colourful world of desert scenery and violent death. But the story was slow-moving, and he was too tired to care about what the characters were doing. Instead, he found himself looking at each scene as a separate story and noticing details in the background – the houses or the hills or the cactus – rather than what was happening at the front of the frame. His attention was only pulled back to the action when there was a killing or a gun-fight. These were bloody and realistic and yet so remote from the real death that he had lived through. What was so amazing was the completely emotionless figure of Clint Eastwood. People were being shot all round him, frequently by him, yet he seemed totally unmoved by each death. He was like a robot, dealing out death without anger or fear. It was so different from Ray's experience and he envied the cold, detached attitude of the actors, it was so purposeful and unswerving. Life would be much easier like that – especially if the 'dead' men could get up and walk away when the scene was over.

From time to time he looked round the cinema and saw that there were only about twenty people in the whole audience. The rain had obviously kept most people at home by their fires. He pictured the scene in his own front room with his family sitting down cosily, not knowing what was going to burst in on them at any minute. He forced the thought away – it was going to be a long evening and he needed to be as calm and remote as the character in the film, so he must relax and gather himself. Eventually, he closed his eyes and just listened to the film, letting the bright colours on the screen filter through his eyelids and jump into his brain shapelessly.

The back of his neck hurt when he woke up, and his ear had been squashed against the hard edge of the seat. The film was still on, and the three main characters were advancing across a graveyard. He looked at his watch – just gone 7.15. He must have been asleep for nearly an hour. His clothes were clammy and his whole body ached with stiffness.

There was some shooting on the screen, and now there were only two characters left to search for the gold. In the last scene, a man was left standing precariously on a wooden grave-marker with a noose strung round his neck and his feet unsteady. It looked as if at any minute he would slip and be left strangling in mid-air. It seemed to Ray, as the thought of what he was about to go through began to grow, that that man's position was very similar to his own. One slip and . . . and now Eastwood was riding off and leaving the man, but at the last moment he turned round and shot the rope, and the man fell to the ground unharmed. Life should be like that.

It had stopped raining when Ray got out of the cinema but a wind was blowing, and all the buildings still dripped. He shivered and went into the phone-box and got out a coin. The police were bound to be there by now, there was no avoiding it. He had to keep tight control over himself and remember all the details that he had worked out. He had only gone out for a twenty-minute walk down to the shops and back on the Wednesday evening. He had not been to the Blackston Road. He knew nothing about a stolen bike. He had not caught a bus at the Angel Roundabout. The conductor must have mistaken him for somebody else. He had jumped off the bus in order to get back to the hospital to see if his grandmother was alive and well.

The evidence against him was only circumstantial – yes, things did appear to point to certain conclusions but they were the wrong conclusions. He was innocent, and if he stuck to that and didn't make any mistakes and didn't allow them to trap him into a confession, then they would never be able to prove otherwise.

The phone rang three times before someone picked it up. As the line cleared, he heard his father's voice, urgent and loud: 'Hello. Ray, is that you? Ray?'

They were there – the police were in his house, and his parents knew. Panic rose in him. He wanted to slam down the phone and run, but there was nowhere to go. His only hope was to stay and stick to his story.

'Ray? Ray, is that you?'

There was something extra in his father's voice, almost like terror, that seemed to sweep the ground away from under Ray's feet. This was worse than he had imagined – it was all going wrong and he sensed that there was something else – something that he hadn't reckoned with.

'Ray. Please, Ray, is that you?'

'Hello, Dad. It's me.'

'Oh God, thank God.' His father's voice called out to someone else. 'It's all right, it's him. He's safe.'

Safe? What was this? What had gone wrong?

'Oh Ray, thank God. Listen, Ray, the police are here. They want . . . we want you to come home. We thought . . . oh God, we thought you were dead. They found a letter, and it said that you were going to kill yourself, and we were so worried, we thought . . .'

The phone slipped from Ray's grasp and clattered down, knocking against the coin box.

The letter. The police must have searched his room and found the letter. All the hopes were gone. Now it was no longer just a case of the conductor identifying him – he could probably have lied his way out of that. But there was no way he could lie about the letter. He remembered what it said – 'I killed Mrs Chalmers. It was an accident. I have decided to commit suicide.' The police would have shown it to his parents – that explained the panic in his father's voice. It was the end – the police had everything they needed.

He had never been running away – it was an illusion. He had believed that he was escaping but all the time he had just been running further and further into the net. All the escape tunnels that he had been digging had finally undermined the ground and it had caved in on him.

He could hear his father's voice, faint and mechanical, calling out to him, and he pulled the phone up by the wire and held it to his ear.

'Ray? Ray?'

'I'm here.'

'What's happened? Oh, Ray, why didn't you tell us? I'm sure it wasn't your fault. We'll work things out.'

'Yes, Dad.'

He could hear his mother's voice in the background. 'Ray, are you all right? Why did you do it?' She sounded almost hysterical, and he heard his father's voice say, 'Sh! Leave this to me', before there was a muffled sound as a hand went over the receiver.

Ray called out, 'Dad. Dad.'

No answer.

He called again, 'Dad.'

'Yes, Ray?'

'Dad – stay there. I'm coming home.'

Twenty-one

He had to wait for nearly half an hour for a bus, and he kept expecting to see a police car coming to pick him up, though he hadn't told his father where he was – merely reassured him that he was on his way home and they were to wait for him. His father had told him again that he believed that it had been an accident and that he wasn't to worry, they would stick by him whatever happened. Ray hadn't bothered to say that that wasn't really the point. He had simply promised that he would come home, and then he had hung up.

When the bus arrived, he got on, and almost laughed to himself when he recognized the possibility of its being the same conductor. But it wasn't. He went upstairs, and sat alone in the back seat.

He had thought only briefly of not going home, of trying to disappear completely – perhaps going down to London and joining the hundreds of others who had a reason for hiding themselves from the past. He couldn't do that – he was too tired, and anyway running had done him no good so far, and things weren't likely to improve.

He traced through the events, as the bus sped along. He thought of Mrs Chalmers, and he looked at himself clearly. He had hidden so much, and now it was all out in the light. There was no escaping it, no denying any of the unpleasant facts about himself any more. He had known them all the time – he had had to live with them, for years before the accident. Now he had reached the dead end, and there was no more running to be done. He had to turn and let his parents see that the inno-cent Ray had died years ago and that this was what he was. In the same way that the accident, and now his discovery, had seemed to consist of various elements heading on a collision course, what his parents were having to face about their son was inevitable, too. All people moved through their lives thinking that they knew where they were going but they couldn't see what events were heading in their direction to alter their course or bring it to a sudden end.

When he turned into his road, the police car was parked outside his house.